Love In Store

'You . . . you . . .' Mayu couldn't think what to call him, she was shaking so much with fright. 'If you ever do that again . . . !'

'It was just a joke.'

'Well, save them for somebody who'll appreciate them. Rebecca's back tomorrow.' She picked up her empty Coke and stomped towards the door.

'Mayu?'

Her name stopped her in her tracks. So he did know what she was called after all. 'What?' she asked more softly.

'Don't forget to put your pinny on.'

She stuck her tongue out at him and turned away. Slowly a sly smile crept across her face.

'Oh, William?' she said, turning back to him.

'Yeah?'

She scooped a piece of ice from her Coke and threw it at him. It ricocheted off his shoulder with a satisfying ping.

'Don't forget to duck!' she giggled, and threw another one at him.

J-17

Love In Store

Just Seventeen

Love In Store

by Linda Sheel

RED FOX

For Andrew

A Red Fox Book

Published by Random House Children's Books
20 Vauxhall Bridge Road, London SW1V 2SA

A division of Random House UK Ltd
London Melbourne Sydney Auckland
Johannesburg and agencies throughout the world

1 3 5 7 9 10 8 6 4 2

First published in Great Britain by Red Fox 1998

Typeset in Sabon by
Palimpsest Book Production Limited,
Polmont, Stirlingshire
Printed and bound in Great Britain by
Cox & Wyman Ltd, Reading, Berkshire

Papers used by Random House UK Limited are natural,
recyclable products made from wood grown in sustainable
forests. The manufacturing processes conform to the
environmental regulations of the country of origin.

RANDOM HOUSE UK Limited Reg. No. 954009

ISBN 0 09 926373 4

♥

Check Out The Specials

It was going to be a great summer! Tessa took the letter out of her bag and checked for the umpteenth time that it still said the same thing. Yep. A week today she started a holiday job at Sullivans' department store. How she'd managed to swing that she had no idea. Perhaps her best mate, Mayu, had put a word in for her.

'Hiya, Tessa, how're you doing?'

Tessa looked up and gave Nerd of the Year a dazzling smile. She'd been multiplying her hourly rate by thirty-seven and had just come to the conclusion that she was going to be rich.

'D'you fancy coming to the pictures with me tonight?' he asked, obviously not able to believe his luck.

I'd rather have my toenails pulled out with a pair

of pliers, thought Tessa, but for once in her life she didn't say it. 'I'm sorry, I'm meeting somebody,' she said, and smiled again. What the heck, a girl could spread a bit of sunshine about every now and again.

'Tomorrow then?' he asked eagerly. His face looked like her aunty's mongrel's did when it was just about to be fed.

'No thanks,' she mumbled, then darted across the road before he could ask her what she was doing three months from now, and pushed open the door of the Pizza Palace.

Mayu, Chloe, and Heather were already sitting at a table in the middle of the restaurant. Tessa glanced quickly in a mirror, smoothed her fingers through her short blonde hair, and walked across to them. Chloe started waving a menu about as soon as she saw her. 'Right! It's pig-out night, tonight. Agreed?'

'Agreed.' Tessa grinned back and sat down next to her at the table. 'Happy birthday, Chloe,' she said, handing her a present. It was wrapped in Thomas the Tank Engine wrapping paper, which was all she could find at home, but Chloe pretended not to notice as she ripped it off.

'Oh wow! Vanilla musk! My favourite! Matching body spray and body lotion. That's great, Tessa. Thanks.'

Tessa held her breath. It was the present that Mayu had given her for her birthday. She hated doing it but she was skint. Once she was working it would be different. She knew Mayu wouldn't say anything but Heather was a different matter. She never really meant to, but Heather had dropped her in it more times than she could remember.

The moment passed and Tessa relaxed. She started planning all the different ways she could pay back her mates for the times they'd forked out for her in the past. Apart from Mayu, they'd known each other since playschool. Heather used to be her best friend because they lived in the same street, but when Tessa's dad moved out and her mum took up with Mark, they moved into his house a couple of miles away. Somehow it had settled into Chloe and Heather being best mates and her and Mayu as best mates, but they still all got on really well. Chloe had gone straight from school into her dad's travel agency, but the rest of them were at college together.

'Take a look at that. I'll fight you for the dark one.' Heather poked Chloe and pointed outside to where two luscious lads were scanning the menu and deliberating whether to come in or not.

'Come on, come on,' she urged. 'Pepperoni pizza with extra mushrooms and a side order of Heather and Chloe. Can't you just feel your mouth watering?'

'The blond one has a seriously cute bum,' said Tessa, leaning back in her seat for a better view.

'You shouldn't be looking.' Chloe put a hand over Tessa's eyes and took a quick peep herself. 'What about Alec?'

'Alec who?'

'Oh, Tessa, you haven't.'

'Oh, Chloe, I have.'

'When?'

'Ten days ago.'

'Nobody tells me anything!' said Chloe as the waitress came to take their orders.

'You've been swanning it in the Algarve for the past fortnight,' Tessa reminded her as soon as the girl had gone. 'What did you expect me to do? Pinch one of my next-door neighbour's pigeons, tie a note round its ankle and see if it could flap its way to the Hotel Splendide?'

'It was the Hotel Villanova actually,' said Chloe, grinning.

'I know. I phoned up to tell you the news but the receptionist told me that Miss Davenport was lying on her belly on a sun lounger beside the pool and couldn't possibly be disturbed at this crucial stage of tanning.'

Chloe let out a squeal of laughter and everybody in the Pizza Palace stopped what they were doing and looked across. Tessa knew that her laugh wasn't her most attractive feature, but at least she didn't sound like a pig being chased by the farmer.

'Why did you dump him?' asked Chloe, when she'd calmed down again.

'I was sick of counting the flakes of dandruff on the top of his head,' said Tessa, pouncing on her pizza as soon as it arrived.

'He was nice. You could have given him a bottle of Head and Shoulders instead.'

Tessa shrugged. 'It wasn't the dandruff, it was looking at the top of his head that put me off.

Welcome to Grantchester – land of the pigmy. I reckon it must be something in the water around here.'

'Well your mother obviously didn't drink much of the stuff when she was having you,' said Heather.

Tessa stuck her tongue out at her before continuing, 'The midwife told her to have a bottle of Guinness a day to build her up. It must have bypassed her and gone straight to me.'

'It's amazing you came out as fair as you did then,' said Chloe.

Tessa stared at her for a moment. It was often difficult to tell when Chloe was joking; she wasn't exactly Brain of Britain.

'Mmm,' she murmured noncommittally through a mouthful of cheese and tomato.

'I wish they would come in.' Heather gazed longingly at the two lads who were still deliberating over the menu outside.

'Must be Librans – they can never make up their minds.' Tessa stood up. She'd had ample opportunity to study the blond lad. He was about five foot eleven, a good inch taller than her. Chances like this didn't happen every day of your life.

'What are you doing?' asked Chloe, as Tessa snatched a couple of menus off the table.

'I'm going to ask them if they've seen the specials. It might tempt them in.'

'You can't do that!' Chloe squealed.

'Watch me.'

'I'll come with you.' Heather got to her feet.

'Chloe should get the other one. It's her birth-day.'

Heather pulled a face but stopped to look across at her friend.

'I'm not going out there,' said Chloe.

Heather shrugged her shoulders. 'Well then,' she said, and followed Tessa.

Tessa's hand was actually on the door handle when she saw the two lads wave to a couple of girls who were running across the car park. 'Would you believe it?' she said to Heather. They did a quick about-turn and walked back to the table.

'God, I feel such a prat! Everyone's looking at us,' said Heather, collapsing on her seat in a fit of giggles.

Tessa glanced around and then raised her voice

for the benefit of a couple of old biddies who were staring at her. 'That's better. Got to stretch the old legs every now and then. Stops the arthritis setting in.'

'Tessa!' Mayu shook her arm to shut her up.

'Well, it's your mother that says I should do more exercise to get rid of some of my energy,' she continued, unrepentant.

The blond lad flashed Tessa a grin as he walked over. He was just as gorgeous close to as he was at a distance.

'Shall we sit here?' His girlfriend pointed to the table next to theirs.

Yeah go on, rub it in, thought Tessa.

He sat down facing her. One blond lock dropped over his eye as he bent to pick up the menu, reminding her of an Old English Sheepdog. Tessa smiled as she speared the chips on her plate. Yeah, he could sleep in a basket at the bottom of her bed any day of the week.

'Tell us about your job then. I thought you said you stood no chance,' said Heather.

Tessa's face lit up. 'I was positive. The old cow that interviewed me must have believed it when I told her it was my life's ambition to work there.'

Mayu started to laugh. 'Mrs Turner,' she said.

Tessa nodded. 'I could hardly keep my face straight the way she went on.' She put down her fork, stuck out her chest and looked down her nose at her mates. 'You must understand, Miss Lewis, that at A J Sullivans we demand total commitment from our personnel. Our customers know that once they enter our portals they can expect a friendly smile and a helpful attitude from each and every member of staff. We pride ourselves . . .' She stopped. Mayu was laughing so much that she seemed about to topple off her chair and Tessa didn't want to miss it.

'You look exactly like her,' choked Mayu.

'Thanks a bunch. She must be nearly sixty.'

'You know what I mean. You've got a real talent, Tess. You should be on the stage.'

Tessa shook her head. 'Nah, too risky. A nice steady job bringing in plenty of dosh, that's what I'm after.'

'Do you think they might have any more vacancies at Sullivans?' asked Heather.

Tessa sprinkled sugar on her cappuccino and watched it dive-bomb through the froth. 'Might have. I'll have a word if you like.'

'Great. Ta.' Heather grinned at her and Tessa smiled back. She stopped abruptly as the lad on the next table smiled at her. She was definitely lad-starved; he was obviously smiling at his girl-friend and it was wishful thinking on her part.

'Do you know what department you're going to be in?' Chloe asked.

'Yeah. I go in on Monday for an induction course and then they're letting me loose on sports-wear. Great, isn't it? I had visions of being stuck in the annexe with the lawnmowers and garden furniture.'

'D'you get a discount?' asked Heather.

'Haven't a clue.'

'Ten per cent,' said Mayu, 'but it's for personal purchases only.'

'Stuff that,' said Tessa. 'What do you want?'

'I dunno, but I'm sure I'll think of something.'

Tessa grinned. 'I'll have a look around and tell you what there is.'

'But you're not a size ten, Tess,' said Mayu.

Tessa shrugged. 'I'll tell them I'm on the waiting list for breast reduction.'

Blond boy almost choked on his drink. Serves him right for listening, thought Tessa. She finished her coffee and put her cup down. 'That was great, Chloe, thanks.'

'We're all going to have a sweet, though?' Chloe said.

'Oh well, if everybody else is.' Tessa picked up the menu and happily waded through the desserts. Chocolate fudge cake sounded yummy. She handed back the menu and stood up. 'I'm going to the loo. Anybody coming?'

Mayu followed her.

'I'm sorry about your present,' said Tessa, as soon as the door closed behind them. 'If I'd had anything else I would have given Chloe that, and I couldn't scrounge any more money off my mum. As soon as I get my wages I'm going to buy myself another gift set exactly the same as yours. I promise.'

Mayu smiled. 'It's OK. I knew you were broke.' She took a brush out of her bag and smoothed it through the thick glossy strands of her hair, then checked her face for non-existent spots. Her mum was English and her dad was Japanese, and she seemed to have inherited the best bits from both of them.

Tessa stood well back from the mirror before glancing at her reflection. If she did it quick enough she didn't look too bad. At least those zits had finally been blitzed. 'Who's ravishing then?' she said, blowing her reflection a kiss.

'You could be a model, Tess,' said Mayu.

Tessa was ready with a sarcastic reply but Mayu, bless her, was being serious. Tessa started to cackle. 'Oh yeah. You can just imagine me prancing down the catwalk in a ballgown by Yves St Laurent, catching my foot in the hem, and flattening half the audience.'

They walked back into the restaurant where a large plate of chocolate fudge cake was waiting on the table for her. 'This looks scrummy,' she said, picking up her fork and trying it before she sat down. 'Whose birthday is it next? Can we come back here again?'

'Would you like another coffee?' Chloe beamed around at everybody as though she'd prepared everything personally. Tessa could imagine her in a few years time as the perfect hostess and wondered vaguely if she'd still be included in the invitations.

Two coffees later, after they'd persuaded Chloe to show them her holiday photographs with the promise that they wouldn't laugh and then had practically wet themselves trying not to, they got up to leave. The people on the next table left at the same time and they jostled each other at the door. Tessa stepped back. It didn't bother her to wait for an extra thirty seconds. You'd think they were giving out Mars Bars to the first ones outside.

Suddenly she felt a hand in the back pocket of her jeans and she whirled around, ready to thump whoever it was trying to nick her money. All she had in there was her bus ticket, but even so.

It was the blond lad. He winked at her and then pressed a finger to his lips. Temporarily lost for words, Tessa watched him saunter out of the restaurant, put his arm around his girlfriend's waist, and walk off.

'Prats!' said Heather as Tessa joined her outside. 'Trying to push us out of the way.'

Tessa dug into her pocket and drew out a piece of paper that the blond boy had pushed inside. 'You can say that again,' she said.

'Prats!' said Heather loudly, and grinned. 'What have you got there?'

'Number one prat's name and phone number.' She threw the paper away in disgust.

Heather let out a gasp. 'The blond lad? I thought you said he was gorgeous?'

'Fancy doing something like that when your girlfriend's sitting next to you.' Tessa shook her head in amazement. 'What a slimeball. If they hadn't already gone I'd have run after them and told her.'

'And they have the cheek to call girls fickle!'

Tessa nodded in agreement. In the distance she saw her bus turn the corner, so she said a quick goodbye to the others and pelted across the road. If she caught this one she'd miss the drunks. What it was about her that attracted drunken old men she couldn't fathom, but even when there were empty seats available they'd come and plonk themselves down next to her and start telling her their life history.

As the bus pulled away Tessa spotted blond boy treating his girlfriend to a tongue sandwich at a bus stop further up the road. Ugh! How could she have kidded herself that he was luscious? That shirt he was wearing was pretty gross as well, she decided, turning away in disgust.

Tessa let out a deep sigh. Where had all the decent lads gone? Surely there must be some of them out there somewhere. She wasn't that fussy, was she?

♥

Where There's A Will . . .

Mayu raced into the restaurant the next day and looked around guiltily. She'd spent twenty minutes this morning helping her mum find her contact lens, and now she was late. Luckily nobody seemed to have noticed. She called hello to Kat, who was sorting out her tables at the far side of the restaurant, and started gathering together the salt and pepper pots from her own tables. It was always her first job of the day to fill these, and she piled them hastily on a tray ready to take into the kitchen.

Would that idiotic new chef be in today, she wondered, as she walked towards the swing door that divided the kitchen from the restaurant. He'd spent the whole day yesterday messing about and flirting with all the waitresses. It was a wonder

Mrs Emmanuel put up with him. He was probably from an agency and only here temporarily or she wouldn't.

She rested her tray on one hand and pushed at the swing door with the other. That was strange. It seemed to be stuck. She pushed harder and it gave way. Mayu had a brief impression of size nine boots before they and their owner crumpled to the floor. Will, the idiot chef, was in today all right. He was lying in a heap at her feet.

'That's not fair! It doesn't count if some moron pushes me over!' he shouted to the head chef, who was standing on his hands against the store-room door. The man weighed about twenty stone, sweat was trickling down his beetroot-red face, and he looked as though he was about to have a coronary.

'You were lucky. I'll give you a return match any time you like.' The chef swung his legs down to the floor, took out a hanky to wipe his face, and walked away.

Mayu put down her tray and stared at the lad she'd just flattened. He hadn't moved and his arm seemed bent at a strange angle. 'Are you all right?'

she asked.

He looked at her for the first time and pulled a face. 'I think I might have done something to my right arm. I can't seem to move it.'

'Oh God.' Mayu dropped to her knees beside him. 'I'm really sorry. Shall I ring for a doctor?'

'No.' He reached out his good hand and grabbed her arm. She didn't like to push him away seeing as she'd been responsible for his accident.

'You won't be able to work if you've hurt your arm,' she said. This was awful. If he was employed by an agency he wouldn't get paid at all.

'It might be all right.' He looked up at her through long brown lashes. His eyes were a deep blue.

'Are you going to try to move it? Is there anything I can do?'

'Maybe.'

'What?' She leaned closer. His hair was the colour of a desk in her dad's study; a rich, polished mahogany. She wondered vaguely if it was dyed. No, probably not.

'You can kiss me better,' he said, puckering his lips and closing his eyes. There was a burst of laughter from above, and for the first time Mayu became aware of the rest of the kitchen staff towering over them and not missing a thing.

'You stupid pig!' she said, and struggled to her feet. Her face was glowing; it was probably the same colour the head chef's had been five minutes ago.

Will leapt to his feet, clutching his arm. 'It's a miracle! I'm cured!' he shouted, and everybody laughed louder.

'What in God's name is going on in here? I'm delayed five minutes and the whole place reverts to a kindergarten.' Mrs Emmanuel, the restaurant manager, stalked into the kitchen and thudded a pile of account books on to the nearest surface. The temperature in the kitchen dropped ten degrees as she glared around at everyone like Vlad the Impaler. Finally her eyes rested on Mayu.

'Just what do you think you're doing in here, Mayu? You have customers, you know.'

'I didn't realise.' Mayu took the opportunity to escape and bolted through the swing door. Luckily her 'customers' was an old lady who came in every morning for a cup of tea. Mayu thought it was probably because she was lonely so she tried to spend as much time talking to her as she could. Today, though, as Mrs Williams talked about her cat, how hot it was at night, and how she was looking forward to visiting her sister in Bournemouth, Mayu found it impossible to concentrate. She was seething with anger. What a stupid trick to play on anybody. He must have spaghetti for brains.

A middle-aged couple walked into the restaurant and Mayu stirred herself. Grief! She hadn't switched on the coffee machine yet. They didn't look the type of people who would happily wait for five minutes while their coffee percolated. She raced over to the machine, switched it on, handed Mrs Williams her bill, then dashed over to the couple. Thankfully, they only wanted a pot of tea and two doughnuts.

She walked over to the urn and picked up a stainless steel teapot. Out of the corner of her eye she saw Will leaning out of the serving hatch, trying to catch her attention. She looked pointedly away. Whatever he was up to she didn't want to know. He was stupid and childish and she hated him. She scrunched two tea bags between her fingers and threw them into the pot.

Just because he was good-looking, did he expect every girl to come running when he snapped his fingers? It had made her sick yesterday watching Rebecca giggling and fluttering her eyelashes every time he poked his head out of the hatch. She wasn't in today; he must be feeling at a loose end without all that adoration.

Mayu picked up the tray of tea and doughnuts and marched determinedly across to the couple. What was wrong with him now? He was pointing down at himself and then pointing across at her. Mayu's cheeks glowed with embarrassment. Was he sick in the head? Normal people didn't go around doing things like that.

'A word, Miss Akira.'

Mayu jumped as Mrs Emmanuel's hot breath hissed down her neck. She was about to hand the man his doughnut but her sudden jump made it launch off the plate and land on his lap instead.

'Good shot!' he said, ignoring his wife's tuts of annoyance.

Mrs Emmanuel was waiting for her on the

other side of the swing door. 'Just how many times must I tell you young girls how important outward appearances are when you're in constant contact with the public?'

About three times every day, thought Mayu, but she kept quiet.

'So why are you improperly dressed?'

Mayu froze. Oh no. Please no. She'd done it once at school and the memory still made her feel weak. Once in anyone's lifetime was enough to walk around with your skirt tucked into your knickers. She looked hesitantly around the kitchen. People were pretending to get on with their work. Not Will though. Oh no, not him. He was staring across at them, lapping up every minute. She stared back defiantly, hating him. No, she didn't hate him. Hate wasn't a strong enough word for the feeling boiling inside her. She detested him. No wonder he'd been making obscene gestures at her. He probably thought she'd done it on purpose to turn him on or something. Grinding her teeth, she lifted her right hand and felt her bottom. Her skirt wasn't caught up on that side so she did the same with her left hand. It wasn't caught there either.

Totally confused, she glanced across at Will and then at Mrs Emmanuel.

'Your apron, Mayu. We issue you with two. One to wear and one to wash so you have no excuse not to be wearing it.'

Enlightenment hit Mayu like a frying pan across the back of the head. She stared shamefacedly at the empty space on her front where the frilly white apron that Sullivans thought their waitresses should wear ought to have been. That was what Will had been doing. He'd been trying to warn her before Mrs Emmanuel swooped. She glanced across at him. He gave a rueful smile and popped more bread into the toaster.

'I must have left it in the cloakroom,' Mayu said miserably.

'And what about these?' Mrs Emmanuel indicated the tray of salt and pepper pots.

'I was going to fill them up.'

'Going to? Going to isn't good enough, young lady. No apron, no condiments, what in heaven's name is the matter with you today? I thought you were one of our more reliable girls. Is there a personal problem I should know about?'

Mayu's head jerked up in alarm. 'No,' she said, shaking it vigorously.

Mrs Emmanuel studied her for a moment, then tilted her head to one side. 'Women's problems, is it, dear?' she asked quietly, but not quietly enough that big ears stacking toast only a few metres away didn't hear. He gave a snort, turned away, and she saw his shoulders shake.

I want to die. Please God, take me quick.

God didn't take any notice. Maybe he'd decided that seventeen was too young, that she had plenty more years of humiliation and embarrassment to endure yet. Behind her, Mayu could hear people coming into the restaurant. When was this woman going to let her leave so she could go and serve them? 'Shall I go and get my apron now?' she asked.

'Not now. They're coming in for breakfast already. Go on your first break. Take these condiments back and fill them up when it's quieter.'

Mayu didn't need telling twice. As she walked back into the restaurant half a dozen heads bobbed up expectantly. Some bright spark in Sullivans had decided that they should do breakfast specials for a bargain price. Mayu wasn't a violent person but if she ever met him she'd definitely be tempted to dismember him. When she'd started her Saturday job nine months ago, there'd been ample time in the morning to prepare for the lunchtime rush, but now there was a constant stream of people queuing for tables until the offer ended at half-past eleven.

Mayu raced over to the first table, took their order, thumped it down on the serving hatch, and hurried over to the next. Where was Vicky? She should have been in by now. She glanced across to the far side of the room where Kat was dashing about like a demented bluebottle. The tables between them were filling up but there was nobody to serve them.

With a martyred sigh, Mrs Emmanuel emerged from the kitchen and began serving. Kat and Mayu exchanged grins. There *was* some justice in the world. All Mrs Emmanuel did normally was buzz about the place like a queen bee, bossing everybody else around.

Being busy took Mayu's mind off what had

happened that morning. She couldn't forget Will entirely. Whenever he handed her a plate through the hatch he would pull a daft face at her or say something stupid. Was he never serious? She was sure he was older than she was, but he acted so infantile.

Half-past eleven came at last. Mayu poured herself a giant Coke, picked up a sandwich, and wrote down in the book what she'd taken. As a perk of the job they were allowed to eat what they wanted at a fraction of the cost to the public.

She pushed open the kitchen door and walked straight through to the fire escape where there were some plastic chairs on a small platform. Fetching her apron would have to wait. At the moment she was gasping for a drink.

'Fresh air!' The metal platform shook as Will jumped outside, tore off his chef's hat, threw back his head, and theatrically gulped in lungfuls of oxygen.

Mayu groaned. If she'd known his break was going to be the same as hers she would have asked for a later one. She clamped her hands around her Coke and sucked on the straw. Unfortunately it caught on the ice at the bottom and gave out a large slurp.

Will grinned but didn't comment. He probably drank like that all the time and didn't think there was anything unusual about it.

'I dunno which prat thought up the idea of these breakfasts but I'd like to get my hands around his neck. If I'd wanted to do conveyor-belt cookery I'd have got a job in McDonald's.' Will picked up his own Coke and clambered on to the safety rail along the side of the fire escape.

Mayu held her breath. Why did boys do such stupid things? They were four floors up. If he slipped he'd kill himself. He settled easily on top of the rail and began drinking. Like a baby, he closed his eyes with satisfaction, as the liquid travelled up the straw and into his mouth.

'Doing the breakfasts brings people into the store. They might buy other things on their way up to the restaurant,' Mayu said, simply so she could disagree with him.

Will's eyes flickered open and he started to laugh. 'You're something else,' he said.

Mayu turned away from the intense blue of his

gaze. She realised that what he really meant was, 'You're a moron,' and she couldn't really disagree with him. Why on earth had she come out with such a ridiculous statement?

'You new?'

Mayu shook her head. 'I started full time last week.'

'That's new.' Before she could explain, Will closed his eyes and bent his head back. A seraphic smile lit up his face. 'I was on holiday last week. Ibiza. Island paradise. With the sun on my face I feel like I'm back there. Sun, sea, and s . . .' He opened his eyes and gave her a wicked grin. 'Sangria,' he continued. 'You been?'

'No.'

'What's your name then?'

Mayu chewed at her bottom lip. She'd read his name on his name badge. He obviously couldn't be bothered to do the same with hers.

'All that partying affect your eyesight?' she said cuttingly.

Will covered one eye and then the other and scanned the distance. 'Nope,' he said, turning back to her.

Mayu glared at him. If they were only one floor up she'd definitely topple him off his perch. 'You just have difficulty with small print, like on name badges?' she prompted.

Will stared at her for a second and then he chuckled softly. God, but he was so irritating.

'Yeah OK, I haven't heard of that one, but I'm game. When do we start?'

'Start what?' He was a total pain in the neck. When he wasn't being irritating he was talking in riddles.

'Hunt the name badge,' he grinned. 'It could be fun.'

'Oh for God's sake!' Mayu looked down at her blouse to point out the badge that always left whopping great pinholes behind in the fabric. All she saw was an unbroken expanse of white.

'Have we started? Can I join in?' Will jangled his boots noisily against the metal.

'It's in the pocket of my apron in the cloak-room,' she said dully. She was a total idiot. The fairies had been in the middle of the night. Because there was no tooth under her pillow they'd taken her brain instead.

'You're no fun.' Will threw his hands in the air in disgust. 'You're not supposed to give the game away like that.'

'You could have told me instead of letting me make a fool of myself.'

He shrugged and leaned back precariously. 'Makes a change. It's usually only me that acts the fool around here.'

'I wish you wouldn't do that.'

'Do what?' He stared at her innocently but leaned back even further.

'It's a long way down.'

'Is it? I hadn't realised.' He twisted to take a look, somehow lost his balance, and toppled backwards.

Mayu screamed, jumped to her feet, and raced over to him. Her help wasn't needed. The top part of him might be upside-down but the bottom part remained exactly where it was.

'That was lucky.' He pulled himself upright again and grinned at her. 'If I hadn't twisted my feet through the bars I'd have gone over for sure.'

'You . . . you . . .' She couldn't think what to call

him, she was shaking so much with fright. 'If you ever do that again I'll push you over myself!'

'It was just a joke.'

'Well, save them for somebody who'll appreciate them. Rebecca's back tomorrow.' She picked up her empty Coke and stomped towards the door.

'Mayu?'

Her name stopped her in her tracks. So he did know what she was called after all. 'What?' she asked more softly.

'Don't forget to put your pinny on.'

She stuck her tongue out at him and turned away. Slowly a sly smile crept across her face.

'Oh, William?' she said, turning back to him.

'Yeah?'

She scooped a piece of ice from her Coke and threw it at him. It ricocheted off his shoulder with a satisfying ping.

'Don't forget to duck!' she giggled, and threw another one at him.

♥

Dish Of The Day

'Hi, Mrs Akira!' shouted Tessa, as she walked into Mayu's house on Wednesday morning. She tossed her trainers to one side and then almost skidded over on the wooden floor of the Akiras' hall. Mrs Akira smiled, and it crossed Tessa's mind to wonder whether she polished the hall more thoroughly than she did the rest of the house just for a laugh. If she did, Tessa couldn't blame her. Living with Mayu's dad, who seemed to have left his sense of humour behind in Japan, couldn't be a bundle of fun.

'She's upstairs, Tessa,' said Mrs Akira, and returned to the kitchen.

'D'you fancy coming for a walk?' Tessa pushed open Mayu's bedroom door and plonked herself on the bed. 'I told Chloe and Heather we might see them in the park. Chloe fancies the lad who does the boats on the lake so that's where they're going. Chloe can't row a boat to save her life. It'll be better than the telly watching them.'

'Oh, I don't know. I don't really feel like going out.' Mayu put down her book and sank back lethargically on the bed.

'Time of the month, is it?' Tessa flicked open one of Mayu's magazines and started reading her stars.

'God, don't *you* start! That's what Mrs Emmanuel was asking yesterday.'

'Were you grumpy yesterday as well?'

'No!'

Tessa stared at her mate's downturned lips. Something was up, but Mayu didn't seem too keen to tell her what it was.

'Mrs Emmanuel. Is she the one that chucked me out that time for standing on the table?'

'Yes.'

'Silly cow. I was only trying to get Sam's balloon back. He would have shut up screaming if I had.'

'Do you mind going to the park by yourself?'

'Yes I do. I wouldn't have come all the way over here if I'd wanted to go by myself. You can't lie on your bed all your day off, Mayu. You'll turn into an old woman. Come on, the fresh air'll do you good.'

'Maybe.' Mayu combed her fingers languidly through her hair.

'Oh for God's sake, Mayu, spit it out! What's the matter with you?'

Mayu let out a deep sigh. 'I got an official warning at work yesterday.'

'No! I don't believe it.' Tessa's jaw dropped open. She was always telling Mayu to lighten up and not be so serious. What on earth had she done?

'Well it's true.'

Tessa was amazed. Mayu was as straight as they came, that's why Tessa was so shocked by what she'd said. 'So what happened? Was it a mistake?'

Mayu shook her head. 'It wasn't a mistake. I forgot to put my apron on in the morning—' She got no further before Tessa's deep laugh boomed around the house.

'Oh well, that explains it. I'm surprised they didn't put you on remand.'

'No, listen, Tessa. It wasn't just that.' Mayu

seemed agitated so Tessa shut up. 'I'd forgotten to fill the salt cellars as well.'

Tessa stared at her, gobsmacked. What was this place she'd just signed up for? 'A hanging matter,' she muttered.

Mayu sighed again. 'But the worst thing was the water all over the fire escape. Someone could have slipped and had an accident. They wouldn't have. It would have evaporated. But that's what Mrs Emmanuel said. She was in a bad mood, you see, because Vicky didn't show up and she had to serve her tables because we were busy.'

'You're not making any sense, Mayu.'

Mayu frowned. 'I'm telling you what happened.'

'Why was the water on the fire escape?' Tessa asked. She settled herself more comfortably on the bed. They could be here all day.

Mayu stared at the ground. 'It was one of the chefs. We were throwing ice cubes at each other.'

'Is he nice?' You had to be careful asking Mayu that question. She always saw the best in anyone and would go out with the type of lad you'd normally cross the road to avoid.

'He's an idiot.'

'Oh.' That sounded promising. Tessa searched her memory banks. She often popped in to see Mayu when she was working, but there was nobody in that restaurant who was the remotest bit fanciable. Still, Mayu's taste was vastly different to hers. It seemed to be one of the reasons they got on so well.

'How many warnings do they give before they boot you out?'

'Three.'

'That's all right then. You're not likely to get any more, are you?'

'But it'll go down on my record, Tess.'

'Oh for Christ's sake, Mayu. Do you think an employer is going to refuse you a job when you finish university because you haven't got a reference from Sullivans?'

A slow smile spread across Mayu's face. 'I'm being too serious again, aren't I?'

Tessa leaned across the bed and gave her a hug. 'Yes, sunshine, you are. Although the bit about the ice cubes shows promise. How old is he?'

'About eighteen or nineteen.'

'Is he good-looking?'

'Yes.'

Tessa considered. With Mayu that could mean anything, but it was still worth checking out. First chance she got. She glanced at her watch. 'So, are we going to see if Chloe and Heather have managed to drown each other or what?'

Mayu got up from the bed and smiled. 'Shall we get a boat as well? It's ages since we've done that.'

'Yeah, OK. We could try ramming them.'

The first thing Mayu heard when she walked into the restaurant the next day was Will's laugh. Was he incapable of being serious? Even when Mrs Emmanuel had been bawling them out he hadn't been able to keep a straight face.

'There you are, Mayu.' Mrs Emmanuel walked over to her, and Mayu checked for the third time that morning that she was wearing everything she should have been.

'This is Diane. She's joining us for the summer. We'll take over your tables this morning while I show her what to do, so you can help out in the kitchen. I'll call you when Rebecca goes for her break.'

Mayu smiled at the girl and said hello. The waitressing Mrs Emmanuel did on Tuesday had certainly upset her; she wasn't going to risk it happening again.

Mayu walked into the kitchen and slipped a plastic apron over her clothes. 'I've come to help. What can I do?' she asked.

The head chef said his usual, that what he'd like her to do wasn't possible in a kitchen, and she waited with her arms crossed and a tight smile on her face until the laughter died down.

'You can give me a hand if you like.' Mayu didn't need to turn around to know who that voice belonged to.

'We're trying out a new dish for lunch and I need a packet of chicken lips from the chest freezer in the storeroom.'

'Chicken lips?' Mayu stared at him, but he didn't look up. He was engrossed in cracking eggs into a bowl.

'Right-hand side, near the bottom,' he said.

Mayu walked into the storeroom, put on a pair

of padded gloves, and opened the freezer. She felt at a disadvantage because her mother wouldn't touch convenience food. They must be a new product, like fish fingers or turkey drummers. Methodically, she lifted out packets of sausages and frozen vegetables and stacked them on the shelf beside her. She came to the bottom but didn't come across any packets of chicken lips. Maybe she'd missed them. She sorted through the pile to check.

'They're not there,' she said, looking up to see Will watching her from the door.

'Must be in the left-hand side,' he said, and turned away quickly.

'Moron,' she muttered, replacing one set of food and starting on the other side. The freezer was huge and she had visions of toppling inside as she reached into the very bottom. There were chicken breasts, chicken legs, chicken drumsticks, chicken wings, and even chicken nuggets, but there was nothing remotely resembling chicken lips. The suspicion that he was winding her up filtered into her brain.

'Haven't you got them yet?' A huge grin was splattered all over Will's face as he walked into the storeroom. The rest of the kitchen staff were gathered in the doorway and were also beaming like idiots.

'They're not in there,' she said, and they all burst out laughing.

'I can't believe you fell for that,' he spluttered, holding his sides, as she piled everything back into the freezer. 'I thought you were brainy and went to college.'

'Who told you that?'

'Nobody. I'm clairvoyant.'

'Clairvoyant?' She slammed the lid of the freezer down. 'That means you can see the future before it happens?'

'Yeah.'

As she passed him on her way to the door, Mayu gave him a swift kick on the shins. 'Well you didn't see that about to happen, did you?' she said.

Mayu was back in the restaurant when Tessa came in. The lunchtime rush was over and there were only a few customers.

'Any chance of a coffee?' Tessa plonked herself on a seat in the centre of the room.

'That's not one of my tables.'

'I know, but I can't see into the kitchen from your bit.'

Mayu groaned. She might have known what Tessa had come in for.

'Call him out then.' Tessa hoovered up the froth from the top of her cappuccino.

'I can't call him out. What do you think he is, my pet Labrador?'

Tessa started to giggle. 'Go on.'

'No.'

'Hey Rover! Walkies!' she boomed out.

Mayu turned away. Thank God Mrs Emmanuel was on a late lunch. Tessa's laughter ceased and Mayu saw that she was staring at the service hatch. She didn't need three guesses to know who had popped his head out.

'My, my, my, that's what I call dish of the day,' she heard Tessa mutter as she picked up her coffee and wandered over.

Ten minutes later she wandered back, and perched on the edge of one of Mayu's tables. 'He's nice,' she said, scraping her finger around the cup to capture the last traces of froth.

'You try working with him,' said Mayu.

'It'd be fun. You should go out with him, Mayu. It would make a change from the boring creeps you usually go for.'

'Thank you, Tessa.' Mayu flicked her with her cloth. Tessa might be her best mate, but she could go too far sometimes.

'Thanks accepted,' grinned Tessa.

'You seemed to be getting on with him OK. I'm surprised *you* don't want to go out with him.'

Tessa shrugged. 'I could tell straight away that he didn't fancy me, and life's too short to waste on lost causes. He was friendly enough, but he was looking over my shoulder all the time we were talking. I reckon he was watching you.'

Mayu snorted. 'If he was then it was only because he was trying to think up new ways of tormenting me.' She told Tessa about what had happened that morning and went off to take table three's money while Tessa was laughing.

'Oh God, Mayu, you really are an idiot. Fancy falling for something like that.'

'Well I didn't know, did I? Your brothers are always eating the strangest things when I come round. Dinosaur- or alphabet-shaped stuff.'

'Yeah, I know, but chicken *lips*. Honestly, girl.'

Mayu bit her lip. She knew exactly what kind of fool she'd made of herself that morning thanks to Will stupid idiot chef. She didn't need Tessa to rub it in.

'I still reckon he fancies you though. He asked me if you'd said anything about him.'

'Oh, yeah, yeah. Give me a break, Tessa. I don't need you winding me up as well.'

'Would I do such a thing?' Tessa demanded with fake innocence, and Mayu laughed.

'Yes.'

'Not this time. I swear to you that's what he said. They're so vain, lads, have you noticed? They think we spend all our spare time talking about them.' She started to giggle. 'I don't know where they get that idea from.'

'What did you tell him then?' asked Mayu, playing along with her.

'I said you had the hots for him.'

'Oh my God, Tessa, you bitch!'

Tessa started to cackle. 'Well, maybe that wasn't exactly what I said. I think it was more along the lines that you kept things to yourself, that you were an enigma – that's a good word, don't you think? That should get him going. Lads love a challenge. They want to be the first to unravel a girl's mystery. And it's true – you are a secretive cow, Mayu. Why didn't you tell me about him before?'

'Why should I tell you about somebody that's about as interesting and as irritating as a midge bite? And he's never been here before on a Saturday anyway.'

'Oh yeah, that's right. He said. He always has Saturdays off because him and his mates go clubbing on a Friday night. That's convenient: he won't interfere with our girls' night out on a Friday.'

Mayu let out a loud groan and threw her tea towel at Tessa. 'This isn't funny any more, Tessa. Do me a favour and shut up about him. And if you ever talk to him again I'd be grateful if you didn't mention me.'

'Yeah OK.' Tessa stood up and slung her bag over her shoulder. 'I take it you didn't read your stars in that magazine you gave me?'

'No. Why?'

'Love is in store for you this month when a dark-haired stranger picks you to be his. Remember that the course of true love never runs smooth.'

Mayu frowned. 'Is that what it said?'

Tessa grinned then shook her head. 'Nah, I just made it up.'

'Tessa!' Mayu grabbed her spray gun, but Tessa was already out of range by the time the shower of detergent spattered through the air. Mayu heard her cackling all the way down the stairs.

♥

Tessa Meets Her Match

Tessa couldn't wait to start work properly on Tuesday. The induction course had bored her out of her head, but as they were paying her to attend she wasn't going to complain. She felt a bit self-conscious in her shop clothes. Navy skirt and white blouse, the letter had said, so she'd thought: great, her old school clothes would do. She'd forgotten how much she'd grown. Her step-dad had told her that she looked like a tart as she'd left the house – they were big on parental support in her family. He did have a point though. Part of her first wages would definitely have to go on a new skirt.

'Tessa Lewis, I presume?' The voice came from behind the till in the sportswear department.

'You presume right,' she said, as she sized up

its owner. About twenty, five foot eleven (what a waste), oil-slick gelled hair, and an overpowering smell of deodorant or aftershave which usually meant with lads that they couldn't be bothered to wash and thought that would do instead.

'I'm Brett Oliver.'

Tessa smiled. Brett Oliver. BO. Nice one.

He held out a clammy paw and as Tessa shook it her smile vanished. He was definitely the type of lad who'd sit next to you on the bus and get his kicks by squashing you into the window every time the bus turned a corner.

'I'm the sportswear department manager.' His chest puffed up with pride.

'Oh? It says assistant manager on your badge. Have you just been promoted?' she asked innocently.

Two red streaks flashed across his cheek. 'Mr Edmonds is on holiday. I'm acting manager.'

'Right.'

'Shall we get you settled in, then? I'll show you around the storeroom while there's nobody about.'

Tessa didn't like the sound of that. Would she

get the sack for headbutting the assistant manager if he tried it on? She considered for a moment and decided she probably would.

'. . . and these are the T-shirts. The main thing you must remember is that everything is stored in alphabetical order . . .' BO's voice was like a bumble bee; it droned on and on. Tessa leaned against the shelves and fought the urge to close her eyes. And she thought the induction course had been boring.

'. . . So Adidas is always stored before Nike, for instance. Do you think you'll be able to remember that?'

'I'll try my best.' Patronising prat! Did he think she had the brain power of an amoeba or what?

'. . . and now the trainers. Same thing here but complicated by the fact we're dealing with numbers as well. Are you listening? This is important.'

Tessa jumped. She'd been thinking about the film they'd all gone to see on Friday night. 'Yes, it's just my way of concentrating.'

BO looked unconvinced. 'I think I'll give you a little test to make sure.'

'Like at school, you mean?'

The sarcasm was lost on him. 'That's right. Men's size ten Reebok "Slice Canvas" trainers. Fetch them please.'

Tessa positioned the stepladders under the right shelf and clambered up. Moron! Him and his fetch. What did he want her to do, shove the trainers in her mouth and come down on all fours?

The trainers were on the very top shelf. She reached them easily, but poor old Mayu would have stood no chance. It had gone quiet below so she glanced down to see what was up. BO was squatted down, tying his laces. From that angle he had a perfect worm's-eye view up her skirt, and she could tell that was exactly what he was doing by the stupid grin splattered all over his face.

Without a second thought, Tessa let the trainers drop. Pity they hadn't been in the electrical department and the trainers weren't a microwave, but they weren't exactly lightweight. They bounced off BO's head with a satisfying thud.

'Ooo sorry,' she trilled. 'I get a bit wobbly on ladders.'

His face was a funny shade of purple as he glared up at her. For a second she was sure he was going to topple the ladders over with her on them. Yeah go for it, she thought. Sullivans might give her a bundle of dosh in compensation.

But he turned and walked away.

'Do you want me to find anything else?' she called after him.

'No,' came the strangled reply from the door.

Tessa clamped both hands over her mouth and the ladders shook with her laughter. What a meanie! He hadn't even told her whether she'd passed her test or not.

It seemed that that was to be the highlight of her day. BO exacted revenge in typical slimeball fashion. Whenever he got the chance he would swoop over when she was with a customer and explain things so painstakingly slowly to her that they must have thought she was on a special needs programme. Most of the decent lads that came into the department seemed to be joined at the hip to their girlfriends, but those that weren't were definitely put off.

Lunchtime came. Tessa gobbled down her sandwiches and went upstairs in search of Mayu. Her mate wouldn't be too chuffed to see her during one of her busiest times, but she had to moan to somebody.

She squeezed herself around a table beside a mum and dad and their kid who looked as though he was in training to be a Sumo wrestler. Mayu gave her a fleeting smile, zoomed past, and returned carrying three plates of chicken dinners that she put down in front of the family. Fat boy pounced on his as though he hadn't eaten for a week, and ripped the flesh from the chicken like a tiger at the zoo. Tessa had to look away. She'd been thinking of becoming a vegetarian for some time and he'd definitely brought the decision closer.

'I can't really talk,' whispered Mayu, coming back with a cup of coffee for her.

'I know. I've just come up to see a friendly face,' she whined pathetically.

'Oh, Tessa, it's not that bad surely? It's only your first day. Once you settle in things will seem different.' She squeezed her arm and Tessa cheered up.

'Maybe. I shouldn't have dropped those trainers on his head. It's really pissed him off.'

Mayu's eyes widened in surprise, but a couple

three tables away were calling her and she had to go. Once she was there they couldn't make up their minds what to have. It didn't seem to bother Mayu like it would have Tessa. Mayu kept a smile plastered on her face while she wiped the table and waited patiently for them to order.

Tessa spotted a free table. She picked up her coffee and nabbed it before anyone else could.

'What are you doing moving around? I thought you'd gone,' said Mayu.

'I had to get away from piranha jaws. You should give him his own trough in the corner.'

Mayu started to giggle and turned her face to the wall so no one could see. 'Shh! Your voice comes out louder than you think, Tess.'

Tessa grinned. 'OK, I'll behave.'

Mayu turned back and cleared the dirty dishes from the table.

'Has he asked you out yet?' Tessa asked, as she spotted Will at the serving hatch.

'Yes. We're getting married next week,' said Mayu sarcastically as she picked up her tray.

'Can I be your chief bridesmaid?' Tessa called after her, but Mayu didn't deign to reply. Tessa leaned back in her seat and watched as her mate manoeuvred her way around the tables. There was something relaxing about watching somebody else work, and Mayu in particular. She made waitressing seem easy and effortless, but Tessa could see what hard work it was. Life in the sportswear department was a doddle in comparison.

As she got up to go, Will's face appeared at the serving hatch and he grinned over at her. She waved back. It was a pity Mayu didn't fancy him at all. She could do a lot worse.

'See you later.' Tessa waved to Mayu as she walked out. She had ten minutes to go to the loo, check her make-up, and go down to the perfume counter where she intended spraying herself all over with the pongiest perfume she could find.

She'd figured out why BO overdosed on the aftershave. It wasn't to hide his body odour but other people's. She knew it was warm outside and people tended to sweat a bit in the summer, but you'd think if they knew they were going to try on trainers they'd change the socks they'd had on for the past month first. The old bloke this morning had been the worst. His big toe had stuck right out of his sock and she could see the dirt encrusted under the nail. The smell was disgusting and she'd been in danger of splattering him with her morning crispies. Funny how BO had kept out of the way when she was serving him.

'There you are.' BO looked pointedly at his watch as she came in, but he couldn't say anything, she had at least three-quarters of a second of her lunch break left.

As she got closer his head seemed to jerk back. This *Midnight in Paradise* she'd tipped over herself was a bit strong. She hoped it would wear off soon; it was making her feel sick.

'Here I am,' she said brightly, standing right next to him. She'd suffered his awful aftershave all morning. They could suffer *Midnight in Paradise* together.

'I'll go for my lunch now.' Coward. He'd said earlier that he was going at two o'clock. 'Daphne is just around the corner. If you get stuck or need anything ring your bell.'

Tessa waited for him to show her for the fifth time that day how to use the bell, but he didn't. He bolted away like a horse at the Derby.

'God, I stink,' she muttered, as the combined fragrance of jasmine, freesia, rose, lavender, and every flower on God's earth drifted upwards. It hadn't smelt so bad in the bottle. It was obviously one that Sullivans kept especially for people like her, who came in to use the perfumes with no intention of buying any. She'd tried washing it off in the ladies afterwards but it hadn't made any difference.

Luckily this department wasn't very busy. She was daydreaming quietly behind the till when her first customer came in. Tessa became rigid. It wasn't fair! He had the body of an Olympic athlete and the face of a male model. He could have done with an extra couple of inches in height, but somehow it didn't seem to matter, he was still drop-dead gorgeous.

'Go away. Please go away,' she whispered, but he took no notice. He walked over to the display of trainers and started looking at them closely as though he meant business. He looked enquiringly over in her direction, but she looked down and pretended to change the till roll.

It wasn't fair! Normally she'd have been over there before he'd made it to the display, pushed him into a chair, and insisted that he try on every trainer in his size. But she couldn't move. If she took three steps in his direction he'd keel over with the smell.

He glanced over again and she ripped the till roll out of the machine. God, she hoped she could remember how to put it back. He'd be as thick as a brick, of course. Lads like him usually were. They spent all their time at the gym and found the instructions on the Coke machine mentally challenging. But if boys could appreciate bimbos why couldn't girls drool over fit lads?

He was looking around to see if anybody else could serve him. Maybe he'd get sick of waiting and come back when she didn't stink. She didn't know why she was getting herself in such a state. He was probably engaged or he'd be so big-headed because of his looks that she'd hate him.

'I'm sorry to bother you, I can see that you're busy.' The voice was deep but surprisingly gentle for someone of his build. Tessa felt really guilty. If somebody had ignored her like that she wouldn't have been so polite.

'These till rolls can be a pig,' she said, closing the lid.

'Aren't they?' His lips curved into a warm smile. 'I worked in a supermarket once. I could never figure the damn things out.'

Tessa smiled back. Close to, he was even more gorgeous than she'd imagined. His hair was a thick glossy chestnut, his skin looked as smooth and soft as her kid brother Sam's, and his eyes were the colour of melted chocolate. Her legs felt a bit wobbly. She leaned against the counter to support herself.

'Do you have these in a size nine?' He placed a pair of trainers on the counter.

Tessa picked them up and looked at them. 'Are these for tennis?' she asked. 'Because the soles are smooth and they won't give you a good enough grip for most other sports.'

He nodded then grinned at her, and her legs wobbled even more. What amazingly luscious lips he had. Imagine those coming in for the kill. 'A girl who knows her trainers. Have you worked here long?'

'It's my first day.'

One perfectly formed eyebrow shot into space.

'Trainers come a close second to football as a subject for discussion in our house,' she explained.

'Oh right.' He gave a deep chuckle. It was the sexiest sound she'd ever heard. If she'd been a Victorian lady she'd definitely have gone into a deep swoon.

'I'm sorry about the smell. I spilt a bottle of perfume,' she blurted out.

'I thought it must be standard sportswear department issue.'

'Say again?'

'To guard against smelly feet.'

'Oh no, nothing like that.' Tessa grabbed the trainers and rushed into the storeroom before he noticed that she was blushing. What was wrong with her? She'd stopped going red when she was eleven.

They did stock his size. Tessa didn't know if she was pleased or not. It meant he would stay longer, but she didn't know if she could lace them up for him without making a fool of herself. Her whole body seemed to be quivering with excitement.

He sat down and began unlacing his shoes when he saw her coming back. His sports socks looked new, as though he'd opened a fresh packet and put them on before he'd come out.

She knelt down in front of him and waited for the immortal words that every male under the age of ninety seemed programmed to say: 'That's where I like to see women – on their knees in front of me.'

They didn't come. 'Yeah, these seem fine. What do you think?' he said instead.

'They look great, but so they should for that price.'

He started to laugh. 'Don't let them hear you saying that. I bet they told you to push the more expensive makes.'

Tessa shrugged. They could tell her what they liked, but she wasn't going to rip off somebody as nice as him.

'I need the support in the more expensive ones for work. It's false economy buying the crap ones.'

'What do you do?'

'I've got a summer job coaching part time at the tennis centre.'

'You're not from round here though, are you?'

He grinned. God, she was doing it again. He'd tell her to shut up and stop being such a nosy cow any minute. It wouldn't be the first time it had happened. But if she was interested in someone she had to know everything about them. Have you got a girlfriend? was the question she most wanted to ask, but she didn't dare.

'I come from Sutton, but I'm going to the university here in October. I came down earlier when I heard I'd got this job.'

'What course are you doing?'

'Physics.'

Physics? Christ! Her mouth dropped open.

He pulled a face. 'I know. It's a complete conversation stopper. Like telling people you're a mortician or something. I'm just a boring git, I'm afraid.'

Boring? Him? No way! Tessa knew that she could talk to him for the rest of her life and never be bored. 'I've always liked physics,' she blurted out.

He started to laugh. 'I don't believe you. Name something you like about it.'

Tessa's mind went blank. She'd hated the teacher, she'd failed the subject at GCSE, and deleted any record of it from her memory banks. 'Er, what I meant to say was that I've always liked tennis.'

He laughed even louder. 'Now, that I believe.' He leaned towards her and smiled. His teeth were white and even, and she stared at them, mesmerised.

Slowly his face moved closer. Sullivans' department store and the rest of Grantchester disappeared. They were the only two people left in the universe. Tessa looked deep into his eyes and she knew that she loved him. This was the lad whose name was tattooed on her soul. It was stupid: he hadn't touched her, he hadn't kissed her, but she knew.

'What does a person have to do to get some service around here!'

Tessa jumped as reality kicked her in the face.

'I've been waiting at the till with this tracksuit for the past five minutes while you've been canoodling with your boyfriend. I've a good mind to report you to the manager!'

Tessa picked up the trainers and stood up. Her

body felt strange – as if she'd just stepped off the Waltzer at the fairground. She tried to walk over to the till but her legs didn't seem to want to move. Her bones had turned to mush.

'Are you going to serve me or what?' The woman shoved the tracksuit in her face and Tessa came slowly to her senses. She clutched the trainers and gawped at the woman until her brain cells reassembled.

'I'm afraid I have to serve this gentleman first.' Tessa put on her best posh voice. 'I was advising him about trainers. He's a professional tennis player and must have the best. How would you like to pay for them, sir?' She pointed her feet in the direction of the till, and this time they behaved themselves and carried her there.

He followed her over, looking a bit shell-shocked. He paid for the trainers, mumbled something that she didn't catch, gave her a last lingering look, and went.

Gone! Just like that! She wanted to leap over the counter and run after him, but the woman was chuntering on again, and she couldn't.

As soon as it was quiet she opened the till and

looked at his cheque. Ralf! His name was Ralf. Ralf Peters. This was the lad she was destined to share her life with. She closed her eyes and smiled. Tessa Peters. Yeah, she could live with that. Would he come back this afternoon? Maybe he'd just popped upstairs for a coffee until the tracksuit terror had gone.

Tessa's senses remained on red alert for the rest of the day, but Ralf didn't return.

He would come in on Wednesday.

But he didn't.

He had to come in on Thursday. Friday was her day off this week. If he came in then he might think she'd left or got the sack and he might never bother coming back.

He didn't come in.

The universe couldn't be so cruel. It couldn't give you five minutes with the lad of a lifetime and then tear him away for ever.

It couldn't . . . or could it?

♥

If You Can't Beat 'Em . . .

'Looking forward to your girls' night out then?'

Mayu paused on her way to the storeroom and stared at Will. 'How do you know about that?'

'Your mate told me.'

Mayu smiled. Tessa was like a radio transmitter. She gave and received more information in a few minutes than anybody else she knew.

'She hasn't seemed so chirpy the last couple of days.'

Mayu frowned. When Tessa was happy it was like a Mediterranean summer. At the moment they were in the middle of an Arctic winter.

'So what's up?' Will persisted.

'Oh you know.' Mayu walked into the storeroom and took down a box of sugar sachets. Tessa's problems were her own business. She would feel disloyal discussing them with anybody else.

Will was scrubbing down his work surface when she came out. 'I don't actually, but it doesn't seem that you want to tell me,' he said, continuing the conversation.

Mayu hesitated. He'd been less obnoxious than usual over the last few days and it had been nice, but mates were mates and she wasn't going to discuss hers with him just to keep him sweet. She turned away.

'So where are you off to tonight, then?' he continued.

'The bowling alley.'

'You go there every week?'

'No. Sometimes we go to the pictures, sometimes to Barney's. If Tessa has to babysit sometimes we all go round there. It depends.'

'I see.' He juggled his spray bottle in his hand like an outlaw in a film juggling his gun.

'I'll see you on Monday then,' said Mayu. She put her hand on the swing door, ready to push.

'I'll be in tomorrow.'

'Are you working overtime?'

'Nah. She's changed my day off to Wednesday for the time being.'

'That's my day off as well.'

'God! Is it? That means I'll have to suffer you for one more day than I need to.' Will took his cloth and threw it in the sink.

Ditto, thought Mayu. 'As long as you try to suffer in silence,' she said, pushing open the swing door. As she did so she tripped on something. It was her apron caught up around her ankles; Will must have untied it while they were talking, and she hadn't felt a thing.

'You seem to have a problem with that pinny.' Will leaned against the work surface and grinned.

Mayu slowly shook her head. He was a total nutter. She bent to pick up her apron. Oh well, if you couldn't beat them maybe there was no option but to join them.

She plastered a sugary smile on her lips and turned back to Will. 'See you tomorrow then. I'll think of you slaving over a hot stove while I'm enjoying myself at the bowling alley.'

'Come again?'

'Tom Sullivans' retirement do. You'd think with

all the money he has he'd have held it in the Ritz instead of here, wouldn't you?'

Will's face was a blank, and Mayu had to turn her face away to hide her grin. She wasn't very good at this kind of thing.

'Mrs Emmanuel offered me double time to stay behind but I managed to get out of it.' Mayu opened the box of sachets to avoid looking at him. 'They're having outside caterers as well, but she said she wanted you to do the carvery.'

'She never said anything to me.'

'Oh God, Will, where's the meat?' His face was several shades paler. Mayu's jaw muscles ached with the effort of trying not to laugh.

'In the freezer.'

'Do you think it'll defrost in time?' she asked, and then just as Will took off his chef's hat and raked his fingers through his hair she spoiled it all by bursting out laughing.

'Why you little . . .' He leaned back against the sink and watched as the tears rolled down her cheeks. It wasn't really that funny; she didn't know why she was laughing so much. Tessa would have done it so much better. She'd have been in the storeroom throwing joints of meat out of the freezer and clattering roasting dishes about, totally straightfaced. But Will's face had been a picture. He'd completely believed her, and it had felt good turning the tables on him for a change.

Mayu looked sheepishly up at him as she wiped the mascara from underneath her eyes, but he grinned and pointed to a plaque above the door – YOU DON'T HAVE TO BE MAD TO WORK HERE BUT IT HELPS.

Mayu smiled back and rolled her eyes. It was beginning to seem like she was already halfway there.

'Did Ralf come into the restaurant today?' were the first words Tessa said as Mayu met her outside the bowling alley.

'How should I know, Tessa? I don't know what he looks like.'

'You'd recognise him if you saw him. That means he hasn't come in.' A dark cloud seemed to form over Tessa's head.

Mayu waved to Chloe and Heather, who were

already on a lane, and they went to change their shoes.

'Come on, Tessa. Try to forget him just for tonight,' Mayu encouraged her as they walked over to join the others.

'You don't know anything about love,' said Tessa dramatically.

'What's this about love?' Chloe stopped sorting balls and turned to listen.

Tessa told them about Ralf.

'And you didn't hear what he said when he went?' asked Heather.

Tessa shook her head miserably. 'No. I think I was only really functioning on auto-pilot, and this old bag kept rustling her tracksuit and tutting so I couldn't hear properly.'

'Maybe he was asking you to meet him outside at six o'clock, and he hasn't been back 'cause you didn't,' said Heather.

Mayu saw the look of horror that swamped Tessa's face, but before she could kick Heather she must have noticed it too.

'No, no, I'm sure he didn't say that. If he did he would have come back to make sure, wouldn't he? He was probably saying, "I'll see you around," but he hasn't been back because he's been working. Yeah, I bet that's it. He'll be in again next week,' Heather gabbled.

Tessa didn't reply. She stared at the ground, her shoulders hunched, and looked as if she might burst into tears at any moment. Mayu hated seeing her like this. In all the years she'd known Tessa she'd never seen her cry, and it just didn't seem right that she should work herself into such a state for a boy who she'd only met for a few minutes and might never see again.

'Look, Tessa, you keep saying how nice he is. Maybe that's all he was doing: being nice,' she said.

'Yeah. How do you know he hasn't already got a girlfriend?' asked Chloe.

Tessa snatched up a ball. For a moment Mayu thought she was going to aim it at them. 'None of you understand!' she said, and stormed on to the lane. She let go of the ball and it hurtled up the middle. The pins dived for cover and Tessa scored a strike. The lads on the next lane applauded. Tessa told them where to go.

'Thanks, pal,' hissed Heather. 'I had my eye on the dark one.'

Tessa shrugged, dropped into a seat, and folded her arms.

'I was supposed to go first,' said Chloe. 'You were second, then Mayu, then Heather.'

'All right. Don't get your knickers in a twist. We'll say that was your score. I'll have another go and then it'll be right.' Tessa snatched up another ball, threw it at the pins as though they were her worst enemies all lined up in one spot, and scored another strike. The lads on the next lane didn't say a word.

They finished their first game and decided to have a Coke. Tessa's mood was affecting everybody, Mayu noticed. Chloe seemed miserable, but maybe that was because she'd been so thoroughly slammed in the game. They all knew that Tessa was the best player among them, but only Mayu knew that she usually dropped a few shots so that she wouldn't win by too much. Tonight, however, she was playing as if she was on a personal vendetta. Their own scores looked ridiculous in comparison.

'So how's your love life, Mayu?' asked Heather jokingly.

'Mayu's OK. The boy of her dreams would come running if she snapped her fingers.'

'Tessa!' Mayu hadn't said anything to Heather and Chloe about Will because she knew what they were like. They'd blow it out of all proportion, just like Tessa had.

'Go on! Spit it out! We want to know every little thing.' Chloe and Heather gathered around her like vultures. She flashed Tessa a look of annoyance, but Tessa was staring into space and didn't notice.

'And speak of the devil,' said Tessa when Mayu had finished. 'Don't tell me – you told him you were coming here tonight. Right?'

Mayu followed her gaze along the lanes to where Will and a group of his mates were parading about and she felt herself begin to blush. She didn't know why. 'He didn't say he was coming,' she mumbled.

'He probably didn't know whether he could persuade his mates to come,' said Tessa.

'The lads on lane ten? Which one is it? That one

with the dark hair is a bit of all right.' Chloe and Heather jostled each other for a better look.

Mayu groaned. Why didn't they just announce it over the Tannoy?

'That lad with the dark hair has just waved. I think he fancies me. I like his T-shirt.' Heather tossed her hair back and smiled in their direction.

'That's Will,' said Mayu.

'God, it isn't! You lucky cow, Mayu!'

'We just work together. I've told you, he's an idiot.'

'Well if there's nothing going on between you, you won't mind if I wander over.'

'Back off, Heather. This one's got Mayu's name on it,' said Tessa.

'Well she must need glasses then because she doesn't seem to have realised.'

'She's just a slow reader.' Tessa turned to her. 'Go on, Mayu, go for it, before somebody else sinks their claws into him.' She stared at Heather, who turned away and finished her drink.

'I'm not going over.' Mayu could just imagine what would happen if she did: he'd start shouting, 'Oh my God, I can't even get away from her in a place like this,' and hide under the chair or something. It was bad enough at work. She wasn't about to set herself up for public humiliation.

'Why not?' demanded Tessa.

Mayu shrugged. 'He's with all his mates.'

'So? It's just moral support. They take the piss out of us and say we can't even go to the toilet ourselves, but they're worse. D'you want me to come with you?'

'No!' All she wanted was for Tessa to shut up.

'What do you think he's come here for?'

'To have a game of bowls with his mates.'

'Oh yeah. As if.'

'You've got love on the brain, Tessa. It's just a coincidence. And I'm not going over and making a fool of myself.'

'Yeah, OK,' said Tessa, and Mayu breathed a sigh of relief. Normally, when Tessa got her teeth into something she was like Chloe's Yorkshire terrier and wouldn't give it up.

'I'll go over and see why he's come. I don't mind making a fool of myself,' Tessa continued, and Mayu groaned. She might have known.

'Don't you dare,' she said.

'Why? You're looking at your fairy godmother, girl. One wave of my magic wand and you can live happily ever after.'

'I'm happy enough as I am, thanks.' Tessa was bad enough trying to be helpful when she was in a good mood. In the strange mood she was in now anything might happen, but it wouldn't be Tessa that would have to live with the consequences for the rest of the summer. Mayu could just imagine how big-headed and overbearing Will would become if Tessa walked over and announced in front of all his mates that her best friend fancied him. It was a ridiculous idea. How on earth had she got it into her head?

Tessa kicked out at a chair with her foot. 'I'm only trying to help. Just because my life's ruined it doesn't mean I don't want you to be happy.'

'Oh, Tessa.' Mayu sat down beside her and gave her a hug. 'I'm sure everything's going to be all right. I bet you a cinema ticket that he'll come into Sullivans next week to see you again.'

'You don't think he's already got a girlfriend?' Tessa asked.

'No.' Mayu had to cross her fingers behind her

back as she said it. It was only a half-lie. She didn't know for certain whether Ralf did or not, and she was saying it for the best of reasons. Tessa just didn't seem ready to face the possibility that she might never see this lad she believed to be her soulmate again.

'I think something special must have happened for you to react the way you have,' she added. She was speaking the truth there. Something special had happened to Tessa, but whether it had also happened to this Ralf person was another matter.

'I knew you'd understand eventually, Mayu.' Tessa stood up and smiled at her. 'Does anybody fancy another Coke before we have our next game? My mum gave me a sub on my wages.'

'I'll come over and give you a hand,' said Mayu. She didn't trust Tessa not to go over to Will and his mates.

'Shall we ask if the lads want a drink?' whispered Tessa as they came close.

'If you like. As long as you don't mind me never speaking to you again,' answered Mayu.

'Meanie,' hissed Tessa.

Tessa paid for the drinks, but as they turned to

leave Will sauntered over. 'Fancy seeing you here,' he said.

'Fancy.' Tessa rolled her eyes and leaned back against the counter.

'Are you having a good game?' he asked Mayu.

'Yes.' Mayu could hear his mates giggling behind her. What was he up to? Her body tensed as she waited for him to try and get his own back for the trick she'd played on him earlier.

Will stared at her for a moment, then took some money out of his pocket and checked the price board above their heads. 'Oh well, see you tomorrow then,' he said, walking past them to the counter.

'Aw, isn't that nice?' said Tessa as they made their way over to the others.

'What's nice?'

'He's shy, bless him.'

Mayu's jaw dropped open. Shy! Will? She'd never met anybody less shy in her life. 'You're mad,' she said to Tessa.

'No I'm not. It's you that's mad. What were you looking at him like he was Jack the Ripper for? No wonder the poor lad couldn't get his words out.'

Mayu shrugged. She was sure she hadn't been looking at him like that. Tessa always exaggerated.

'He's not as good-looking as Ralf of course, but he's still bloody gorgeous. Don't you think so?'

'I've never said he wasn't good-looking,' said Mayu. In fact she hadn't realised quite how good-looking he was until tonight. She was so used to seeing him in his white chef's overall and stupid hat that it was a shock to see him in jeans and T-shirt.

'Mad, mad, mad,' muttered Tessa, as they walked back down the steps to the bowling lanes.

♥

Ralf Goes Window Shopping

On the way to work next morning, Tessa stopped
at The Card Shop and bought Mayu one of the small
pottery animals that she collected. She thought
she'd been a bit moody last night and this was
by way of saying sorry. She'd give it to Mayu at
lunchtime and she'd also ring Heather and Chloe
to apologise. They were good mates. Not many
would have put up with the way she'd acted earlier
last night.

She took the stairs two at a time on the way up
to the sportswear department. It was the start of
a new day. Perhaps Ralf would come in. But if
he didn't she hadn't got to let herself get in such
a state about it. Lads weren't worth it. No, that
wasn't true; this one was. But she mustn't take it
out on other people.

'Any messages?' She bounded into the stock-room and gave BO a huge grin. It confused him when she was nice to him. You could see his little brain ticking over.

'What do you think this is, some kind of hotel?'

'You know what I mean. Did anybody come in looking for me yesterday?'

'Like the police, you mean?'

'Ha ha very funny. Have you ever thought of being a stand-up comedian?' That was her quota of being nice to him for the day. 'So did anybody ask for me then?'

'The only person who's been asking for you is the assistant store manager. She wants you to help the window dresser today. I'm to tell you that you'll find her in the window beside the side entrance. So I'll bid you farewell.'

'I want to stay here.' If she moved, Ralf would definitely think she'd left, and they'd never see each other again.

BO started to laugh. 'I'm touched, but as they say: tough. Mr Edmonds is back on Monday and we've the Saturday lad in today. We don't need you.'

Tessa tramped down to the side window with a heavy heart. It put on a few extra tons when she saw what she was supposed to help with. Bridal Wear! Whose idea of a sick joke was that?

'Hi! You must be Tessa.' A bright bubbly blonde, who looked as though she should be hosting a game show, smiled at her. Tessa smiled back. It wasn't her fault she was five foot three, slim, and had hair straight from a Pantene commercial.

'I'm Catriona. I'm so pleased you're tall.'

'Are you? I'm not.'

Tessa heard the tinkling of tiny bells. It was Catriona laughing.

'You can pin these garlands of silk flowers along the line on the wall behind you. It's just out of my reach.'

Tessa picked up the flowers and glanced out of the window. Now she knew what Herbie, her brother's goldfish, felt like. 'Doesn't it get on your nerves people gawping in at you all the time?'

Catriona shook her head. 'You forget they're there most of the time. You're a student, right? Is this a Saturday job or are you here all summer?'

As they worked Catriona chattered constantly.

It was quite a shock for Tessa to find someone as nosy as she was, and she took to her instantly. Catriona was right: the people outside soon faded away. Catriona's tales of how she and her boy-friend had hitched around Europe when they left college were much more interesting.

'Have you seen the Sellotape anywhere? I can't get this veil to stick on Cynthia's head.'

Tessa grinned. 'Do you give them all names?'

'Of course. I even talk to them when nobody's here. Present company excepted, you get a lot more sense out of them than most people at Sullivans.'

'I think I saw it in the corner. Hang on a minute, it's rolled behind Davinia here. If I just bend—'

'No, Tessa!'

'It's all right. I've nearly got it. I just need to stretch a little bit more.'

'Tessa, get up! You're showing your knick-ers!'

'God, I forgot where I was.' Tessa straightened up and turned gingerly to look out of the window. A double-decker bus had pulled up outside. Please God, don't let there be anyone on it from college.

Please let it be a busload of grannies on their way to bingo.

God had packed his case and gone on his holidays. The first person she saw, his eyes as wide as saucers, was Ralf.

Tessa staggered out of view and banged her head methodically on a hardboard dividing wall.

'Hey, come on, it's not that bad.' Catriona raced across and stopped her. 'They were nice knickers – very tasteful.'

'What's he going to think now?' Tessa moaned.

'Who?'

'Ralf. The lad I was telling you about, the one who bought the tennis trainers. He was on the bus.'

'Oh my,' said Catriona.

'The first time I saw him I stunk to high heaven, and the second time I was flashing my knickers. What's he going to think?' she wailed. 'It's a total disaster.'

'No,' said Catriona. 'Of course it isn't,' but she didn't sound that convinced.

*

'I can see the headlines in the *Echo* tonight,' squealed Chloe. 'Shopgirl strips in Sullivans! Read all about it.'

Tessa's expression didn't alter.

Mayu had hoped that Chloe and Heather coming into the restaurant would cheer Tessa up. She'd lightened up last night, but now she was sitting in the corner eating her lunch, throwing off mess-with-me-and-you're-dead vibes. It seemed that short of presenting Tessa with a giftwrapped present of Ralf Peters, nothing was likely to penetrate her gloom.

'Your mate's going to bop the other one in a minute,' said Will, as he handed her two plates of spaghetti bolognese.

Mayu sighed. Tessa wouldn't, but she was likely to say something she'd regret for a long time. She served the spaghetti then zoomed back to the corner.

'Have you seen this figure that Tessa got me?' she asked, hoping to change the subject. 'A kitten in its basket. Isn't it cute?' She offered up a prayer that Heather wouldn't spot it was the same as one she already had. Luckily she didn't.

She left them cooing over the kitten and hurried over to a table where three lads were trying to attract her attention by snapping their fingers. She took their order, trying not to let it show how much she detested it when anybody did that. It seemed harder work today: a restaurant full of customers *and* Tessa to keep happy.

'Will?' Mayu didn't leave the order on the counter as she normally did, but waited until he strolled over.

'What can I do for you, lotus blossom? Shall we leave all this behind and take the next flight to Ibiza?'

'I wish,' she said with feeling. 'How much have you got in your piggy bank?'

He pulled a face. 'Not enough.'

'Table three want to know how hot your curry is.'

He smiled, and she noticed a dimple on his cheek for the first time. It made him look incredibly cute. 'How hot do they want it?' he asked.

'I quote: "We don't want the mild muck we had last time."'

Will poked his head out of the hatch, glanced over in the lads' direction and grinned. 'I can make it hot.'

Mayu was getting to know that grin. 'They're customers, Will. Don't do anything stupid.'

His grin widened. 'As if.'

'Caterpillars,' she reminded him. A girl who'd dumped his brother had practically screamed the place down when she'd found a giant specimen snoozing happily under a lettuce leaf on her plate.

'Curried caterpillars,' he mused. 'Difficult ingredient to get hold of, but a master chef always has a jar handy next to his station. Now if they'd wanted woodlice . . .' He went away laughing.

Mayu turned away. She'd have to hope that he was only joking. He could lose his job otherwise. She went back over to her friends.

'He's lovely, Mayu,' said Chloe. 'Has he asked you out yet?'

Mayu groaned. 'I've told you there's nothing going on between us,' she said. She wished they wouldn't keep going on about it. She wished that he *would* ask her out, so then she could say no, and then they'd be satisfied and shut up about it. But he *wasn't* going to ask her out, was he? If he'd wanted to he'd had plenty of opportunities.

'I think I'll just wander over and say hello.' Heather glanced at Tessa to see if she'd stop her, but Tessa was currently inhabiting a different planet to the rest of them and didn't say a word.

As she hurried about, Mayu caught snatches of their conversation. 'So you go to college one day a week on day release? That's great. I'm surprised we haven't seen you in the refectory. Yeah, the stuff they serve up is a bit crap. I wouldn't eat there either if I had the choice. When does your course start again?'

Mayu polished the table next to them and realised that she was rubbing so hard she was almost taking the surface off. So Will went to their college, did he? Nice of him to tell her.

She walked over to Chloe and Tessa's table. 'Has Tessa gone?' she asked.

Chloe nodded. 'I don't know why she's making such a big deal about it. It's the type of thing you expect Tessa to do – show her bum to everybody in the window. Normally she'd be the one who laughed most about it.'

'One of Will's mates fancies me like mad. I said he could ring me.' Heather returned to the table, her cheeks glowing.

'Which one?'

'I'm not sure.' Heather wrinkled her brow in concentration. 'I'm trying to remember what they looked like. None of them were really gross, were they?'

'Depends what you mean by gross,' said Chloe.

Mayu left them to it. Trouble was brewing on table three.

'Will!' she shouted through the hatch.

'Oo, I'm so much in demand today,' he said, putting on an effeminate voice.

'Table three are complaining about their curry.'

He grinned. 'I thought they might.'

'You didn't put caterpillars in it, did you?' she whispered.

He started to laugh. 'What do you think I am? I did go a bit overboard on the chillies and cayenne pepper though. Give them their money back. That should shut them up.'

'They're demanding to see somebody.'

He sighed. 'OK, I'll send Alistair out. He owes me one.'

'It should be you. You did it. You should take the blame.'

He gave her a strange look and then grimaced. 'Well normally I would, but as I went to school with two of them I think they might twig the moment they clocked me that it wasn't an accident. Give us a break, Mayu. They're total losers. I've been waiting to get my own back on them for a long time.'

'All right. I'll tell them somebody will be over to see them in a minute.' She went over to their table to clear their dishes. As she picked up a plate her hand froze. Was that half a caterpillar or a chewed-up chilli on the side? She put it hastily on her tray. She couldn't be sure and she didn't really want to know.

'What type of lads does your mate Heather go for?' Will joined her on the fire escape as she took her last break of the day. The coffee tasted stewed but she drank it anyway. She needed the caffeine.

'Ones with two legs,' she said, and then grimaced. What was wrong with her? She wasn't normally so bitchy. 'I'm sorry, I meant she has no particular preference.'

He laughed, and clambered up on his perch. 'It's been like a zoo out there today. At one point I felt like standing at the hatch and throwing the plates out like frisbees. I might do that on my last day.'

Mayu felt her heart thud down to the ground. 'Are you leaving?' she gasped. Suddenly she realised how much she would miss him if he went and how dull her job at the restaurant would be.

'Would you miss me if I did?' he teased.

'Like a hole in the head,' she said, and he laughed.

'I keep applying for better jobs, but until I get my qualifications I don't think anybody's going to be interested. One of these days I'll have my own restaurant. I might give you a job if you ask nicely.'

'You didn't tell me you were on day release.'

He looked at her closely and then shrugged. 'You never asked.'

'Which of your friends liked Heather?' She decided to change the subject. She suspected her voice had started to whine and she didn't like it.

His brow furrowed in concentration. 'I think it'll have to be Andy.'

'You mean you made it up?'

He looked for a moment like a little boy who'd been caught stealing Smarties.

'Why?'

He shrugged. 'To get her off my back.'

Mayu stared at him in amazement. 'Why?' she asked.

Will jumped down from the rail and the platform reverberated under his feet. 'Because some of us have work to do and can't stand around all day chatting and entertaining.' He continued on into the kitchen.

Mayu frowned at his back. Was she going mad? Wasn't that exactly what he seemed to enjoy doing whenever he got the chance?

She took her cup through and stacked it in the

dishwasher. Will was leaning out of the serving hatch and she could hear Vicky's giggles from the other side.

Mayu was totally confused. It was true that lads were a mystery. And this particular one was more of a mystery than any other.

♥

Fragile – Handle With Care

Tessa waited in Mrs Turner's office to hear which department was going to be the lucky one to have her that week. She hadn't realised that they intended moving her from one to the other. She might be doing a stint with the garden gnomes yet.

'Chinaware, dear. Second floor. Tell Mrs Butler I sent you.' Mrs Turner put down her phone and smiled brightly across her desk at Tessa.

Tessa nodded and walked out, wondering whether she'd still be smiling later that day. 'Tessa's the name, demolition's the game,' she muttered, running up the stairs to the second floor. When she was little and they'd come into Sullivans to buy an ornament for her gran her mum had pinned her arms to her side and marched her straight through to the counter, hissing, 'Don't you dare touch anything!' Even now when she went round with her mates she always got the feeling that she shouldn't really be there.

'Are you Mrs Butler?' she asked the woman behind the counter in the china department.

'No, thank God.'

Tessa smiled. This woman seemed OK. She'd be able to get on with her all right.

'We call her Mrs Bustler around here. Don't take it personal, but she probably won't let you serve anybody. She seems to think that everybody's entitled to the whole history of Wedgwood even when they've just popped in for a Peter Rabbit egg cup.'

'I'll tell her I'm studying modern china at college. I am actually, in business studies, only it's the country and not the teacup variety.'

The woman laughed, but shut up quick enough when a well-padded grey-haired dragon emerged from a door behind her.

'Miss Lewis?' Mrs Butler came over and frowned at Tessa. She looked pissed off with her before she'd even started.

'Tessa.' Tessa tried to smile at the woman but her lips couldn't quite manage it. She had the feeling that she probably looked as though she was about to break wind.

'Miss Lewis.' The woman wrinkled her nose as though Tessa had actually done so.

Tessa was dying to say 'Tessa' again and see how long it would go on for, but she'd had her first pay packet and quite fancied seeing the next one.

'I'll go and get started in the stockroom then, shall I?' The other woman winked at Tessa behind Mrs Butler's back and walked away.

'What would you like me to do?' Tessa attempted another smile and managed to look a little less constipated.

'Dust.'

Dust! Tessa studied the woman to see whether she was joking. Nope. No joke had ever passed those lips.

'Mrs Curtis will show you where the cleaning utensils are kept.' She pointed over to the stockroom.

Oh fun! Oh joy! Tessa went in search of dusters. She thought she'd got out of stuff like this by working. Not that they were that hot on dusting in her house anyway.

'Mrs Curtis, show this young lady where the cleaning utensils are kept, if you please,' Tessa said to the woman in the stockroom, and was pleased to see her jump. Yeah, she had the old bag's voice just right. Maybe a fraction too high.

'Jesus! I thought you were her. I was just about to have a sly fag.'

'Oh sorry. What's with this Miss and Mrs stuff anyway? I thought somebody like her would want to call us by our first names; it usually makes them feel superior.'

'She's probably frightened somebody would start calling her by hers.'

'What is it?'

'You promise you won't let on?'

'Promise.'

'Fanny.'

Tessa took a moment to digest this information before she started to laugh and the crockery on the shelves began to rattle. Mrs Curtis shoved a feather duster into her hands and pushed her back through the door.

The minutes ticked by like hours. Monday mornings were usually quiet, according to Mayu, but this was like working in a mausoleum. Whenever anyone hovered at the edge of the department and looked as though they were thinking of coming in, Fanny bustled over to them. This usually gave them such a fright that they charged off in the opposite direction. Tessa felt like leaping out at them shouting, 'I'll head them off this way,' but she'd lasted two and a half hours without breaking anything and had decided to go for three.

Tessa had lunch, did her best not to moan too much to Mayu, and came back to the china department. What exciting job would Fanny have lined up for her this afternoon?

It was dusting duties again. Tessa had a sinking feeling that when she'd finished everything Fanny would send her back to the first lot and tell her to start all over again.

'This stick should have a government health warning printed on the bottom of it.' She waved the feather duster at Mrs Curtis as she passed carrying a basketful of Crown Derby.

'Yeah. Dusting can seriously affect your brain

cells,' she said before Tessa could. 'At least you're only here for the week, love. I'm here for life.'

The woman's words cheered her up. She'd already made a conscious decision to try and put Ralf out of her mind, but what Mrs Curtis said seemed to put things in greater perspective: her life could be a lot worse.

'Hello again. You get about a bit.'

Even if she'd been blindfolded Tessa would have recognised that voice. A rush of blood swept through her body, her hand shook, and a Royal Doulton figurine almost dropped out of it. She'd developed psychic powers: she'd thought of Ralf and he'd appeared!

'Oh hi,' she mumbled. That dusting had done its damage. Where was all the sparkling repartee she was famous for? Wherever it had gone it didn't have a chance to come back before the Mighty Bustler pounced and dragged him off to her lair beside the till.

'And what is it you're looking for, young man? A christening present? Well you've come to the right place. Have you anything particular in mind?'

Tessa listened as Fanny went through her spiel.

It wasn't her imagination, she was sure it wasn't, that Ralf kept looking over in her direction and smiling. He bought a silver money box in the shape of a teddy bear and paid extra to have it giftwrapped. Tessa thought it was the best christening present in the world.

Finally he was free and Tessa's heart started booming. She knew he was going to come over and she just wished that she didn't look such a prat flitting about with her feather duster.

'I hope he likes it. It's for my sister's kid.' Ralf held up the Sullivans' black and gold bag and smiled. Her insides turned to marshmallow, and it was all she could do to stand. Nobody had ever affected her like this, not even after a marathon snog at the pictures.

'I saw what you bought. I think it's lovely,' she managed.

'Really?'

'Yeah, really.'

'Miss Lewis! Go and help Mrs Curtis in the stockroom please.'

'Right.' Tessa turned back to Ralf.

'Now!'

'I better go.' Ralf stuck his present under his arm, gave her a last heart-stopping smile, and walked away.

Evil bitch! Miserable cow! Tessa marched over to Mrs Butler, silently mouthing a litany of abuse. She gripped the handle of the feather duster and knew exactly where she wanted to shove it. Mrs Butler gave her a tight smile as she stomped past. She looked the happiest she'd done all day; destroying other people's lives definitely agreed with her.

It didn't take Tessa long to calm down. Ralf had come in. That meant he could come in again. And he would. You couldn't send out a smile that singed another person's nerve endings and not like them a tiny bit. He'd be back, and this time she'd have her wits about her. She'd tell him straight off what time her break was and the evil old witch wouldn't be able to do a thing about it.

Tessa was flitting about with her feather duster like the sugar plum fairy when Fanny came over to her just before closing. 'Are you enjoying your work in the china department, Miss Lewis?' she asked with a frown.

Tessa gave her a gushing smile. 'I love it, Mrs Butler.' That should upset the old bag.

'Then I'm afraid I have some bad news for you. The toy department is under-staffed and Mrs Turner wants you to report there tomorrow.'

Luckily she turned away before she saw Tessa's reaction. The feather duster hit the ceiling, did a few frantic pirouettes, and narrowly missed a display of glass birds before Tessa caught it.

'Yes!' she said, throwing it up again. Life was good and getting better by the minute. As far as she could see the one and only advantage of having a little brother was that you got to play with his toys. She would have a whale of a time in the basement, and there'd be no Sam hanging on to her and whining that she wouldn't give him a go.

And Ralf would find her. He'd already said how she got around, so he'd be expecting her to be somewhere else next time he came in. And lads were big kids. Once he saw her in the middle of train sets and construction kits he wouldn't be able to resist joining her.

Yeah, she'd play stickle bricks with him any time he asked her.

'I hope you'll be happy with us, Tessa. I like to think we're one big happy family down here.' The toy department manager shook her hand and beamed at her.

Tessa grinned back. The man must be nearing retirement but he was a real sweetie. Fat and jolly, he was probably dressed up at Christmas as Santa. He looked as though he'd be in his element sitting in a grotto with loads of kids climbing all over him.

'So if you wouldn't mind helping Marlon this morning, that would be wonderful. He's over there pricing up jigsaws.' He pointed vaguely to the far corner.

Tessa walked over, smiling to herself. Would she mind? He was so funny. What would he have done if she'd said she did?

She passed a Sylvanian farmhouse and crouched down to look at the figures inside. She'd bought Sam the squirrel family for his last birthday because she'd fancied playing with them, but he'd chucked them away and said they were a pooey present. It looked as if she'd be able to play with them to her heart's content here.

Where was this person she was supposed to help? What had the manager said his name was? Marlon? God, she hoped it wasn't Marlon Baxter, the biggest prat in their college. He'd be in his element here: he had a mental age of about nine.

There were the jigsaws and a pricing gun lying beside them. Perhaps Marlon was round the corner. Tessa took a look just as the most hideous green scaly monster leapt out at her. As its red-veined eye peered menacingly at her, she let out a blood-curdling scream that Mayu would have heard on the top floor.

'Dear, dear, what's going on?' The manager padded over and started to chuckle when he saw them. 'Naughty, naughty, Marlon,' he said, patting the monster on the shoulder and padding off again.

Tessa waited until he'd gone and her blood pressure had dropped from cardiac arrest before calling Marlon something a little more colourful than 'naughty, naughty'. Bloody Marlon Baxter.

She might have known her luck was too good to last.

He ripped off the mask and grinned. 'I got you though, didn't I?'

Tessa gave a bored sigh. 'Try to act your age, Marlon, not your shoe size,' she said, but he was oblivious to sarcasm.

'You were really scared,' he laughed. 'Wait until I tell the lads about it.'

'I wouldn't if I were you.'

'Why not?'

'Because then I'd have to tell them what Angela White told me when she was going out with you, and I don't really want to because it was said in confidence.'

Marlon stared at the ground and kicked out at a pile of Trivial Pursuit with his foot. 'Yeah OK,' he said, and she had to turn away to hide her grin. What a lucky shot! First day of term she'd get Angela in the cloakroom and find out what had happened.

The day passed like a dream. Tessa kept pinching herself to make sure she wasn't going to wake up and find she should have been in chinaware with

Fanny Bustler, she was enjoying herself so much. Most of the time she even forgot to feel irritated with Marlon. Parents seemed so pleased that she was prepared to open toy boxes and show them what the things inside did. She even challenged one dad to a race on a space hopper and they made it as far as the Wendy house before he fell off.

'I've found my vocation. I'm going to pack in college and open a toy shop,' she joked to Mayu at lunchtime.

Marlon was putting some battery-operated animals on a table beside the till when she got back. 'Take a look at these!' he shouted.

'Oh yeah!' She watched the display of penguins, ducks, dogs, and bears all bumping into each other, and started to laugh. One bear had fallen over and couldn't quite right itself. It was stopping a duck from getting past, and every couple of seconds the duck would let out a loud quack as though it was telling the bear not to be so stupid and to get up. Over in the corner, a penguin had got stuck, was nutting the table, and looking totally pissed off about it. The star of the show, though, was definitely the dog. It walked a couple of steps forward, gave a little bark, stood on its hind legs and then did a complete back flip.

'Oh, I want to take you home with me.' She picked the dog up. It had the cutest face and lovely soft fur.

'Will you take me home instead? I'm fully house-trained.' Marlon dropped to his knees and raised one hand like a paw.

'Nah, you can't do tricks.'

'Wanna bet?' He checked behind him, gave a little woof, and flipped back.

Tessa started to laugh. 'Idiot,' she said. 'Where did you learn how to do that?'

'Junior gymnast, I was,' he grinned. 'Even made it to Wembley one year.'

'Clever doggy.' She bent down and patted his head.

He stuck out his tongue and started to pant.

'Nutter.'

'I need a good home. Don't let them take me back to the pound,' he said, leaping up. He took her off balance and she toppled backwards.

'Get off, stupid!' She tried to push him off as

he leaned over her, panting in her face, but he was heavy and she couldn't shift him.

'Oh sorry,' she heard a voice above her. 'I was looking for one of those activity things for babies.'

The voice was familiar. Marlon leapt to his feet, giving her a clear view of its owner. Never had she seen anyone looking as gobsmacked as Ralf did as he stared at her sprawled on the floor. But then she hadn't taken a look in a mirror at herself.

Anyone For Tennis?

'I've managed to change my day off. I told them my gran had been taken into hospital.' Tessa came rushing into the restaurant at five o'clock that night.

'Tessa!' Mayu was shocked. 'Your gran's been dead three years.'

'Yeah, well, she won't mind me lying about her, will she? So, d'you fancy a trip up to the tennis centre tomorrow morning?'

Mayu took off her apron and folded it. She thought Tessa was mad. From what Tessa'd told her about what had happened in the toy department this Ralf lad would probably run a mile if he saw her. 'Don't you think it might be better to wait for a bit?' she asked.

'Like he's going to forget he saw me flat on

my back with that half-wit Baxter slobbering all over me?'

'No, but—'

'I've got to get this sorted, Mayu. I can't think of anything else.'

'You don't know he'll be there tomorrow. You said he only worked part time.'

'I've got to try, Mayu. I've got to let him know that's there's nothing between me and Marlon. If you don't want to come then I'll go by myself.'

Mayu looked at Tessa's determined expression and sighed. How could you tell your best friend that you thought she was about to make the biggest fool of herself ever?

'I know what you're thinking, Mayu.' Tessa sat down on a table and kicked out at a chair. 'I don't care. It's too important. I know he's the boy I want, and if I let him slip away without doing anything I'm going to regret it for the rest of my life.'

Mayu gave her a quick hug. 'Of course I'll come with you,' she said. Apart from anything else, Tessa would need her to pick up the pieces afterwards if anything went wrong.

Tessa jumped down from the table and grinned. 'Thanks, Mayu. I'd do the same for you. Are you all ready? Shall we go?'

Mayu put her apron in her bag. 'I'm ready.'

'Don't look so worried. Everything's going to be great. I know it is.' Tessa walked towards the stairs, rested her bum sideways on the handrail and hurtled down. She waited until Mayu caught up with her. 'Then all we have to do is get you sorted and we can live happily ever after. You're going to have to say something to him, you know. You have to let a lad know how you feel about them. It's the only way.'

'Maybe,' said Mayu, although she had absolutely no intention of doing so. Agreeing with Tessa was often the only way of shutting her up.

Mayu was still eating her breakfast the next morning when the bell rang. Usually nine o'clock meant ten o'clock with Tessa, and Mayu hadn't hurried herself.

'God, I'm so nervous.' Tessa took off her shoes and threw them down. 'My heart's on hyperdrive.'

She followed Mayu into the kitchen. 'Have you left that?' She picked up Mayu's toast and started eating it. 'I couldn't eat a thing before I left the house and I feel a bit sick now; I thought I was going to puke on the bus. I better use your loo before we go as well. Shall we have a coffee before we go or shall we get one there?'

'Calm down, Tessa!' It was making Mayu feel dizzy watching Tessa pacing backwards and forwards in the kitchen. 'You're getting yourself in a state and you don't even know whether he's going to be there or not.'

'Yeah, you're right. D'you think I should ring up and check? No, they might put me straight through to him and I wouldn't know what to say. I need to see him face to face. Although—'

'Deep breaths. Now!' Mayu grabbed Tessa's shoulders, and for the next few minutes made her breath rhythmically in and out to the sound of her counting.

'OK.' She let her go.

'That stuff really works, doesn't it?' said Tessa, taking a few extra breaths for luck.

'Yes it does, but we'd better go now while you're

feeling the effects. We'll go to the ladies when we get there and we'll do the same again.' With any luck it might stop Tessa looking and behaving so manic that it scared the poor lad off for good.

They got to the tennis centre twenty minutes later, and with Tessa as calm as she was ever going to be they headed for the reception. The bloke behind the glass partition barely lifted his head as Tessa gasped out her request.

'Peters? No, it's his day off,' he said, and returned to filling in his form.

'Are you sure?' Mayu felt Tessa sag, and she kept a tight hold of her arm.

'Sure? Of course I'm sure.'

'Ralf Peters?' demanded Tessa, and Mayu tried to pull her away. She could see the bloke beginning to get annoyed.

'Watch my lips. Ralf Peters. It's his day off today. Is that clear enough for you or do you want me to repeat it again?' he said.

'Moron,' said Tessa, and turned away.

'Sorry, she's a bit upset,' said Mayu apologetically.

'She'll be more than upset if she doesn't stop

kicking that pot plant,' said the man, rising to his feet.

'Tessa!' Mayu dragged her away. 'Let's go upstairs and have a coffee. We can think about what you're going to do next.'

'Like jumping off the roof you mean?' said Tessa as she tramped upstairs. 'Oh God, Mayu, I got myself all worked up for nothing. I'm so stupid.'

'No you're not.' Mayu pushed her into a chair by the window and went over to order their coffees.

'If he had been here it would have been all sorted by now. It's not your fault he wasn't,' Mayu said when she came back.

'I should have rung up to check,' said Tessa, 'but I was so sure he would be here. I'm not so sure of anything any more. Everything's gone wrong. Maybe somebody's trying to tell me something.'

'Like the course of true love never runs smooth, you mean?'

Tessa groaned, but Mayu was pleased to see a faint smile on her face.

'So that's plan A down the drain. What's plan B?'

'I never got that far,' said Tessa. She took a few

sips of her coffee and then her face lit up. 'I'm going to write him a letter! That's probably better than seeing him face to face anyway. It means I can explain everything properly without getting embarrassed about it.'

'Right,' said Mayu guardedly.

'Have you any writing paper in your bag?'

'Mmm. I've got a full set of envelopes too.'

'Great! Let's have them.'

'I was joking, Tess.'

'Oh.' Tessa took a deep swig of her coffee and stood up. 'I better go and see if I can find some then.'

Mayu settled back in her chair. There was a good view from here over the outside tennis courts and she became interested in one of the matches being played. One of the lads had the same hair-style as Will and she found herself hoping that he would win.

'Brain food,' said Tessa, returning ten minutes later with two huge plates of double chocolate gateau. 'I couldn't resist them when I walked past.'

'That's not brain food.' Mayu picked up a spoon and smiled.

'Course it is. It'll be converted into energy, won't it? And that's what my brain needs at the moment – plenty of energy.'

'Did you get some paper?'

'Sort of. That miserable old git was still on the reception so I knew I'd be wasting my time trying to scrounge any off him. I asked him for an application form instead. I'll have to write on the back of it.'

It took Tessa an hour to compose her letter. Mayu continued watching the Will lookalike match and made Tessa spill her coffee by clapping when he eventually won it.

'I feel shattered,' said Tessa. She put her letter into the envelope, scribbled out the name of the tennis centre and wrote Ralf's name on the front. 'I hope Misery Guts is off the desk by now,' she said, standing up.

But he wasn't.

'He's probably been sitting there since the centre opened and people have forgotten all about him,' said Tessa.

'Shh!' said Mayu. The man was already eyeing them suspiciously, and didn't seem at all pleased with the liberties Tessa had taken with his application form.

'If I ever turn out like that when I'm older, do me a favour and shoot me, Mayu, will you?' said Tessa, as they walked out of the centre and crossed the road.

Mayu sighed. It had been a long morning.

'I wonder if he'll ring me or come into the shop?' said Tessa.

'I don't know, Tess. Whatever he does you're going to have to try to be patient.'

♥

Mayu Crashes Out

Patience, unfortunately, was not Tessa's middle name. From nine o'clock the next morning she was bubbling with expectation that Ralf would come into Sullivans to see her. She raced home and set up vigil beside the telephone to wait for his call. But as the days passed and it looked likely that Ralf had been abducted by aliens, because there was neither sight nor sound of him, Tessa seemed to fold in on herself.

On Thursday morning of the next week, Heather came into the restaurant and slumped over a table. 'A bottle of whisky and a tall glass,' she said, when Mayu came over.

Mayu wiped the table while she waited.

'Yeah OK, a cappuccino, but sprinkle plenty of chocolate over the top.'

'You've been down to see Tessa.' It was a statement rather than a question.

Heather nodded. 'She's doing a roaring trade in euthanasia kits.'

'Don't, Heather. She can't help being upset.'

'She could try a bit harder. Honestly, Mayu, you walk down the steps to the basement and the vibes hit you in the face. It's a wonder the kids don't run away screaming.'

Mayu grimaced. She didn't need anybody to tell her the effect Tessa was having on everybody.

'I could never stand that stupid Marlon lad but I feel quite sorry for him. He followed me out and asked if it was anything to do with him, the way Tessa was.'

'Poor Marlon.' Mayu went off to make Heather's coffee. She felt mean for thinking it, but she was truly grateful that Tessa was still in the toy department and hadn't been moved to the restaurant this week. Things were brilliant for her at Sullivans. Since she'd taken Tessa's advice and lightened up a bit with Will they were getting on great. Waitressing used to be something she only did for extra money, but now she found herself looking forward to coming to work and she didn't think she'd ever laughed so much. If only poor Tessa could be so happy.

'We'll have to think of somewhere better to go this Friday. Somewhere that might cheer her up,' said Heather.

Mayu thought for a moment. 'What about Barney's? It doesn't matter if we don't talk that much because the music's loud, and we might even get Tessa up for a dance.'

'Yeah OK. Anything has to be better than last week.' They fell silent. Like her, Heather was probably remembering last Friday's fiasco. Tessa had insisted on keeping her promise of taking them all out for a meal and they'd gone to a Chinese restaurant. Chloe had summed up the general feeling afterwards by saying that she'd had more fun at her gran's funeral, and she'd really loved her gran.

Mayu served two customers and came back to Heather. 'How did you get on with Andy?' she said, remembering.

'All right.' Heather's face brightened. 'He wants to take me to the pictures on Sunday. I'll probably go. It was funny though,' her forehead creased into a frown, 'he seemed to have the impression that I was mad keen on him and not the other way round. It pissed me off a bit to begin with.'

'Oh well, you know what lads are like,' muttered Mayu vaguely, and zoomed off quickly to serve someone else.

As she passed the serving hatch she did a double-take: an orange furry animal was waving at her. 'Hello, Sooty,' she said, waving back. A little boy had left the glove puppet in the restaurant yesterday. If Ladbrokes were taking bets on who had their fingers inside it she could have made a fortune.

Mayu stacked her salt and pepper pots on a tray. She hadn't had time to fill them this morning, and, as her tables were empty at the moment, she decided to do it now. The fact that Will was in the kitchen and she hadn't seen him for a while didn't enter into her decision. Of course it didn't.

'Are you looking forward to your holiday? What time's your flight?' she said to Kat as she walked past. Kat was off to Majorca and had talked about nothing else for weeks. Mayu loved travelling. So why didn't she feel envious? It was strange, but at this moment, she'd rather be in grotty old Grantchester than anywhere else in the world.

'Remember to send us a postcard,' she said, as she pushed open the kitchen door.

A sense of unease hit her immediately. Everybody was standing around. Nobody was doing any work. Her eyes darted across to who they were looking at.

'Mayu!' Will's voice was a muffled croak. He was slumped over the sink. 'Go away! Don't look!' he said, turning his head to her.

'What?'

'I've had an accident.'

'An accident?' she repeated. Her knuckles were white as she gripped her tray.

'I was carving some meat and I was carrying on a bit.'

All the blood drained from her body. She was icy cold. She couldn't move.

'I think it's deep.' He turned slowly towards her and lifted his arm to show her the wound.

His overall was one huge pool of red as his life blood seeped relentlessly into it.

The crash of broken crockery echoed around the kitchen. 'No, Will, you can't die,' she said, as she followed it to the ground. A black swirling pit had opened in front of her and swallowed her up.

'That's it, keep your head down between your knees,' was the next thing she heard as she surfaced from the scary blackness of the pit.

'Will!' Every atom of her body seemed to scream out his name. How could she have fooled herself that he meant nothing to her? Why had it taken until now, when it might be too late, for her to realise how important he was?

'He's going to be all right, love.' It was the head chef, leaning over her, firmly pressing her head down.

'No! All that blood!' He was lying to her, trying to keep her calm. She struggled upwards, needing to know exactly what had happened.

'Just tomato sauce, love.'

Mayu stared at him blankly. What was he talking about? Will was badly injured. He might be dying.

And then she saw him. Apart from the others, his hands thrust deep into his trousers and his head hung low on his chest. 'I'm sorry,' he mumbled. 'It was only a joke.'

'Joke!' Mayu scrambled to her feet and grabbed hold of a work surface to support her. She took a deep breath and then, for somebody who never swore, gave a performance that would have impressed even Tessa's step-dad.

There was a deathly silence afterwards. People stared at the floor, at the sink, at the food mixers, anywhere but at her.

'Mayu . . .' Will stepped forward, but she ignored him. She also ignored the fact that there were thirty-five minutes left of her shift as she stormed out.

♥

Double Depression

It would get better. Soon it would get better. All the magazines said it would. But it didn't.

Tessa smeared blueberry eyeshadow around her eyes and wondered if she should do everybody a favour and not go out tonight. If she was brave and noble that's what she'd do, but she wasn't. She needed her mates. She needed to be with them, doing normal things, pretending that things were the same as they'd been before she met Ralf.

She finished her make-up and flexed her jaw muscles in an attempt to smile. It had been a long time and they seemed to have forgotten what to do, but she tried again and this time she managed it. She'd read somewhere that if you were miserable and you smiled at yourself in a mirror your brain thought you were happy and sent out happy chemicals into your bloodstream. This fooled your body into thinking that you were happy and you cheered up automatically. Tessa stared at the idiot grinning at her in the glass. It was a load of bull.

She picked up her bag, hurtled downstairs, and slammed the front door. There was probably an article she hadn't read that would tell her that dancing was the ideal solution for a broken heart. She was probably about to prove that one wrong as well.

Why hadn't Ralf been in touch? She'd explained everything in the letter. Did he have a girlfriend after all and when he'd got her letter he'd thought – my God, who *is* this girl? Couldn't he even pass the time of day and be friendly with someone any more without them jumping to the conclusion that he fancied them? Tessa added humiliation to her list of sufferings.

Chloe and Heather were waiting in the queue outside Barney's. Tessa joined them, ignoring the complaints behind her. 'Hi!' she said, fixing a smile on her face. She really must try tonight.

'Is Mayu coming?' asked Chloe.

Mayu? Why shouldn't she be? Tessa looked blank and then her smile froze. Mayu! She'd gone up to the restaurant to see her today and they'd told her she'd phoned in sick with a stomach upset. God, she was a selfish self-centred horrible cow! She'd completely forgotten to ring up and ask how she was.

'Er, the line was engaged and I couldn't get through,' she mumbled, and she saw Chloe and Heather exchange glances. They knew she was lying, and Tessa felt even more ashamed.

Mayu appeared while they were brushing their hair in the cloakroom. 'How's your tummy?' asked Tessa. She'd have to be extra nice to make up.

'There was nothing wrong with it,' said Mayu.

Tessa's mouth dropped open. What was going on here? Mayu never lied. She'd never skived off school or her job in her life.

'Didn't you tell her?' Heather asked.

Mayu shook her head.

'Tell me what?' demanded Tessa.

They all stared at her. Eventually Chloe sighed. 'I'll tell her,' she said.

'What a stupid prat!' said Tessa when Chloe had

finished. 'You must have been in a hell of a state, Mayu.'

'Not that you'd care.' Mayu unfastened her make-up bag and rummaged inside. Tessa had known her long enough to know that she was deeply hurt.

'Of course I care, Mayu. You know I do,' she protested.

'That's why the phone never stopped ringing all day with you phoning up on your breaks to see how I was.'

'I'm sorry.' She was the lowest of the low. Mayu had every right to be pissed off with her.

'I know it's difficult phoning from work some-times, but I thought when you got home . . .'

'I'm sorry,' repeated Tessa. She didn't even try to make excuses this time.

'And I'm sorry that you're so wrapped up in your own problems that you can't spare a second for your supposedly best mate.'

Tessa stared at the floor. Whenever she'd needed Mayu her mate had always been there for her, but today when Mayu had needed her she'd let her down. True friends weren't only there for the good times. Mayu, Chloe and Heather had proved that. They'd stuck with her while she was a total pain. She didn't deserve it.

'You're right. I shouldn't have come.' Tessa picked up her bag and walked out of the cloakroom. The music vibrated through her bones as she pushed her way through the crowds to the exit. A bouncer grabbed her hand, and she didn't have the energy to stop him as he stamped it with a re-entry pass. She lowered her head and walked miserably past the people in the queue outside.

'Hello,' said a voice from one of them.

'I shouldn't have said that to her.' Mayu sat down on a chair in the corner of the cloakroom and felt miserable.

'Of course you should. She's got to learn that she's not the only person who matters in this world,' said Heather.

Mayu shook her head. 'She doesn't think that.'

'Well, she acts like it sometimes. She's been a pain in the bum for months.'

'Days,' said Mayu.

'It's felt like months,' said Heather.

'It hurt a lot that she couldn't be bothered to phone me.'

'Of course it did.' Chloe patted her shoulder. 'You were right to tell her. Maybe it'll make her snap out of it and come back to planet Earth again.'

'Too right,' said Heather. 'I tell you, I nearly put an advert in the *Echo* this week: Will the individual known as Ralf Peters please contact Tessa Lewis currently working or pretending to work at Sullivans' department store, and put us all out of our misery.'

Mayu gave a weak smile. Tessa had been in the wrong but she knew she was sorry. She didn't like to see her upset like that. 'I think I'll go and find her,' she said.

'She's probably already on the dance floor,' said Chloe.

'I think she's gone home.' Mayu checked her watch. She should be able to catch Tessa before her bus came.

'Good luck,' she heard Heather say as she hurried out of the cloakroom.

'Hello, Tessa,' said the voice again, and Tessa looked up. For a second everything went out of focus and all she was aware of was Ralf's face smiling at her.

Smiling?

Laughing, more like. Embarrassment and humiliation saturated every cell of her body. The things she'd said in that letter! If only she'd taken Mayu's advice and waited until she was thinking more clearly. Tessa noticed his mates grinning at her. Oh God, had they read it as well? She could imagine them rolling around on the floor, practically wetting themselves, as they quoted bits of it to each other.

'Hello,' she said, and turned away. She was dying inside but she wasn't going to let them see that. If any of them said anything she'd say that one of her mates had sent the letter for a laugh.

Why hadn't he replied? Why had he been so cruel? There was no sign of a girlfriend with him, but she supposed that didn't mean anything. This was Friday night. She was probably out with her mates while Ralf was out with his. Tessa lowered her head and hurried her pace.

'Isn't it any good in there tonight, then?' Ralf left his mates and started walking along with her. Why was he bothering being nice? If he was that nice a person he would have rung her up the first day and told her she'd made a mistake instead of letting her hang on for days, hoping.

'It's all right,' she shrugged.

'But you're not?'

She glared at him. If he'd actually bothered to read her letter properly he'd know that she wasn't all right. Was he getting some kind of kick out of this? 'Don't worry, I'm fine,' she hissed. 'I'm well and truly over it now.'

'You've broken up with your boyfriend then?'

'What boyfriend?'

'That prat, I mean that lad you were on the floor with in the toy department at Sullivans.'

'Marlon? He's not my boyfriend. You know that.'

'Do I? And how am I supposed to know? He looked pretty much like a boyfriend to me. Or do you carry on like that with any lad who takes your fancy?'

'Oh just get lost, will you!'

Ralf came to a standstill and stared at her. Tessa stared back. It would be the last she'd ever see of him so she might as well take a good look. Why was he so gorgeous? Why did she still want him so much it hurt when she obviously didn't mean anything to him?

Slowly, he shrugged his broad shoulders. 'If that's what you want,' he said quietly, and turned away. It felt as if he'd ripped out her heart and was dragging it along the pavement behind him.

'You could at least have had the decency to read my letter!' she shouted.

He stopped, turned, and frowned at her. 'Letter? What letter?'

'The one I sent to you. The one you couldn't be bothered to read.'

'What address did you send it to?'

Tessa stared at him in disbelief. Was he pretending? Was there a chance he hadn't received it? 'I didn't actually send it. I left it at the tennis centre for you,' she said.

'You came all the way up to the tennis centre to leave me a letter? Wow!' Ralf's frown disappeared and a slow smile took its place. Tessa's brain fizzled and popped like a cereal commercial as all the nasty thoughts she'd had about him were wiped out.

'Who did you leave it with? Don't tell me. I bet it was that old bloke on the main desk who wants to bring back hanging for driving offences?'

'Sounds like him.' Tessa smiled back. Ralf had left his mates. He was standing here, talking to her. He had to like her a little bit, hadn't he?

Ralf leaned against a lamp post and shoved his hands into his jeans pockets. 'Tell us what was in the letter then.'

Tessa's cheeks simmered gently. 'Every time I've seen you I've been doing something stupid,' she said.

'Mmm,' he agreed, and her cheeks reached boiling point.

'I was looking for the Sellotape when I was in the window and I forgot that everybody could see what I was doing. And Marlon was pretending to be a battery dog when you came into the toy department. He'd just knocked me over and—'

Ralf started to laugh, and a warm glow spread through her body. It started at her toes. 'You're so funny, Tessa,' he said.

'I can be hilarious if I really put my mind to it,' she mumbled.

'Funny's OK for starters,' he said. Tessa watched his lips. He had the most amazing smile. He could be on a toothpaste advert.

'How did you know my name?' she asked, dragging her eyes away.

'I read your name badge. How did you know mine? I presume you did if you wrote me a letter.'

'I read your cheque.'

He laughed again, and reached out for her hand. It disappeared into his great masculine paw, and Tessa felt safe and small at the same time. It was an amazing sensation. She didn't want him ever to let go.

They walked for a while. Tessa didn't have a clue where they were going and she didn't care. In fact she couldn't feel her feet on the pavement. Ralf was probably the one who was walking and she was just floating after him. Somehow they ended up in a shop doorway – Millets Outdoor Leisure. For the rest of her life it would have a special significance.

'You still haven't told me what was in your letter,' he grinned. 'Was it how great I was and how much you fancied me?'

Tessa cringed. It hadn't been far off. She was pleased now he hadn't got it. 'Big-head,' she said. 'I was asking for advice on my backhand.'

He started to laugh. He was standing so close now that she could feel his breath warm against her cheek.

'I haven't been able to get you out of my head, Tessa,' he said, becoming serious, 'but I thought I was wasting my time. I didn't want to muscle in if you already had a boyfriend.'

'I've thought about you quite a bit as well,' she said, and his hot-chocolate eyes crinkled at the edges.

'You've got lovely hair.' He reached out a hand and pushed a strand gently away from her face.

'It's a mess.' Why hadn't she washed it before she'd come out tonight?

'Then I love messy hair,' he said, and she grinned. She'd never met anybody as nice as him. Ever.

'And you have a lovely smile,' he said, tracing his finger around her lips.

Tessa started to tremble. His closeness was doing funny things to her, invading all her senses. His touch was tickly and sent prickly little shivers running down her spine. His voice was deep and mellow; she could listen to him reading her mum's Kay's catalogue and it would be like listening to poetry.

'You smell lovely,' she whispered. His aftershave mingled with the smell of soap and shampoo. It was as if he'd just stepped straight out of the shower. The thought of it did weird things to her stomach.

'Thanks,' he said. 'And you smell a bit nicer than you did the first time I met you as well.'

'That's why you couldn't get me out of your head – it was the smell.' Tessa started to giggle. She was feeling so tense; she needed to relieve the tension somehow.

Ralf put his arms around her waist. She shut up as instantly as if he'd flicked a switch. This was it! Any second now he was going to pull her towards him and kiss her. Blood thundered around her system. She was so nervous. It was as if nobody had ever kissed her before.

'I wanted to kiss you the first time I saw you,' he murmured. 'If that woman hadn't started ranting on about her tracksuit I think I might have made a fool of myself.'

'I wouldn't have thought you were a fool.' Tessa twined her arms around his neck. She needed the support. If he didn't kiss her soon she was going to pass out.

At last, his strong arms gripped her to him and held her against the taut muscles of his chest. His lips felt smooth and warm as they pressed against hers, and he kissed her more thoroughly and expertly than she'd ever been kissed before. Every other snog had simply been a trial run for this moment. A beautiful warmth flooded her body; it felt as if her insides were turning into runny honey.

A lifetime later, he lifted his head and smiled.

Tessa was beyond words. If this was a film they'd be standing beside a waterfall and there'd be fireworks and rockets crackling in the sky behind them. She had to make do with Millets' shop doorway, but she didn't mind. She didn't want to be anywhere else in the world but here with Ralf at this moment.

Tessa was in love.

♥

Sorry

'I'm sorry for going on and on. Am I being really selfish? It's just that I'm so happy. I wish you could feel the same way, Mayu.'

Mayu smiled across the bed at Tessa. Happy wasn't the word. Tessa looked as though she'd been plugged into the mains and was sparking with vitality. Her skin glowed and her hair shone. If she was a dog and they entered her for Crufts she'd win Best of Breed award for sure.

'I'm really pleased for you, Tessa. He's lovely.' It had been a shock finding them wrapped around each other in a shop doorway on Friday night, but he hadn't seemed put out by her interrupting them. He'd seemed keen to go back to Barney's and meet Tessa's friends. Chloe and Heather had been green with envy after he'd talked to them.

'What are you going to do, Mayu?'

'About what?' Mayu crossed her legs more tightly underneath her. She knew exactly what Tessa was talking about.

'About you know who.'

'I don't know,' said Mayu miserably. 'I can't bear to think of him laughing about how stupid I was.'

'I'm sure he hasn't been laughing, Mayu. I bet he's more embarrassed about it than you. For one thing, you could have cut yourself to pieces falling on top of all that broken crockery.'

'I suppose.' Mayu twisted the corner of her bed-spread between her finger and thumb and sighed deeply. 'I really thought he was dying, Tessa. I made such a fool of myself, but when I saw him like that I couldn't help it. I've never been so frightened in all my life. I hate him.'

'You don't hate him, Mayu. If you did you wouldn't have reacted the way you did.'

'No, you're right.' Mayu picked at a loose thread. 'I didn't realise how much I'd grown to like him and how much he meant to me until I thought I might never see him again. But how could he do that to me, Tess? It was awful.'

'I know, but I'm sure he never meant it to turn out the way it did. I'm sure he really likes you, Mayu.'

'Then why did he do it? It was such a horrible thing to do.'

Tessa shrugged her shoulders. 'I don't suppose he really thought about it beforehand. He just did it. Lads are like that. You've seen the wildlife programmes where the male of some species parades about doing really stupid things just to get the female's attention.'

Mayu frowned. 'So you reckon it was some kind of courting ritual?'

'Oh God, Mayu, I don't know.' Tessa threw up her palms in surrender. 'It was probably meant to be a joke. He's probably like me: it seems a good idea at the time and it's not until you're actually doing it that you realise what a stupid half-brained idea it really is. Remember when I tipped that bottle of Fairy Liquid into the fountain on the roundabout by Tesco's?'

Mayu remembered. 'But that was funny, Tess.'

Tessa grinned back. 'Yeah, I know, but what I'm saying is that it didn't happen the way I thought it was going to. I expected it to lather up and there'd be a few bubbles blowing around. I didn't expect that whacking great tidal wave of foam frothing all over the road, the police having to stop the traffic, and all those letters in the *Echo* about bringing back corporal punishment for juvenile delinquents.'

'No,' said Mayu, laughing. It was good to have the old Tessa back again.

'What are you going to do then?' asked Tessa, and Mayu stopped laughing. Her mate was like a summer cold: difficult to shake off.

'I'm not sure.' She stared out of the window, away from Tessa's steady gaze.

'But you are going in tomorrow?'

'Probably.' Mayu stared at the clouds scudding across the sky. She didn't want to tell Tessa that she was thinking of ringing around other restaurants to see if they needed waitresses. She'd call her a coward, and she'd be right.

'OK. I'll come here first and we'll go in together.'

'Why?'

'Because I owe you, Mayu. You're a good mate and you've put up with a lot from me over the last couple of weeks.'

'It's stupid you coming here first, Tessa. I'm not a little girl.'

'No. A little girl would hold her mummy's hand and do exactly what she was told. You had no intention of going in tomorrow, did you?'

'I hadn't decided.' Mayu shifted uncomfortably on the bed.

'You have to face up to things when they happen, Mayu. It's no good running away.'

'Hang on. Don't I usually say things like that?'

'Yeah, you do. So it must be true. Right?'

Mayu was no more decided when Tessa turned up next morning and practically frog-marched her to work. At least she got Mrs Emmanuel over straight away.

'Are you all better, dear? Nasty things these tummy bugs. I'm sure you didn't contract it here. I always tell all my staff to be extra vigilant in the hot weather.' And that was it. No mention of her going off early on Thursday or of the broken salt and pepper pots. She glanced across at her tables. Somebody had set new ones out. She wondered who it was.

Mayu walked down her row, checking her tables, taking sugar sachets from one to put on another. Any other time she'd have gone into the storeroom for another box, but she wasn't setting foot in that kitchen unless she had no other choice. So much for facing up to life.

'Hi, Mayu, you OK?' Vicky's voice wasn't its usual squawk, but soft and gentle, the way you talk to people with terminal illnesses.

'I'm fine, thanks,' she said, trying to stop her fingers trembling. This was awful. She shouldn't have come in. And she hadn't even seen *him* yet.

It got worse. Everybody was treating her as if she was a glass ornament that was about to drop off its shelf. Vicky told her she'd missed her, and Rebecca must have had a personality transplant because she started helping her with her tables when it got busy.

Mayu did her best to avoid Will. She waited until his head disappeared from the hatch before she grabbed her plates, and if she looked up when he was watching her she looked the other way. He looked hurt, but he'd hurt her a lot more than that on Thursday. She didn't go outside for her break as she normally did but sat in the corner of the restaurant to eat her sandwich and drink her Coke. Was she being childish? She wasn't sure. All she knew was that she couldn't make herself go through that swing door and face him.

One roast beef dinner and one chicken and mushroom pie for table six. They should be ready now. She walked over to the hatch to check. Yes, they were waiting. She slid the beef dinner on to her tray, trying not to spill any of the gravy, and picked up the chicken pie. Something caught her eye. Something was written on top in thin coils of pastry: *Sorry*. And then there was a round circle with two dots for the eyes, a small blob of pastry for the nose, and a thin strip turned downwards for an unhappy mouth.

Mayu glanced into the kitchen. Will was watching her. He mouthed the word 'sorry' and then pointed two fingers at his head and pretended to blow his brains out.

Too confused to know what to think, Mayu automatically picked the pastry off the pie and delivered it to table six. With any luck the bits that remained looked as though they were meant to be there.

Ignoring table five, Mayu walked straight into the kitchen. If Will had anything to say she was ready to hear it now. He was standing beside his station, his shoulders hunched. He hadn't seen her come in, and her breath caught in her throat: he looked so sad that she wanted to rush over and hug him.

'Mayu!' His face brightened, and before she knew what was happening he'd grabbed her and a chair and dragged them both into the storeroom where he closed the door and wedged the chair against the handle.

'What on earth are you doing?'

'I'm kidnapping you.'

Mayu groaned. Nothing had changed. He'd said sorry for one joke so he thought it was OK to play another one.

'Don't be so stupid.' She reached out to pull the chair away but he stood in front of it, blocking her. His face was serious. He didn't look as though he was joking.

'Let me go, Will,' she said slowly.

'Just a couple of minutes, Mayu, please. I tried to get your address from personnel but they wouldn't tell me, and I rang directory enquiries for your number but you're ex-directory. I was going out of my head in case you were so pissed off with me you didn't come back to work.'

Mayu stepped back from the door, her mind reeling as it tried to assimilate what he was saying. She was wrong about him; he must care about her to go to so much trouble.

'Thanks.' He gave her a fleeting smile and all the anger she'd felt seemed to melt away. Her stomach churned as she waited to hear what he was going to say. She hadn't felt this nervous since she'd taken her GCSEs.

Will took off his chef's hat, threw it into the corner, and raked his fingers through his hair. 'God, I don't know where to start. I've rehearsed this over and over in my brain, but my mind's a blank now I've got you here.'

'Why?'

'Why? I don't know why. Will Armstrong – Grade-A loser, that's me.'

Mayu rested against a shelf of pickles. She didn't know what to say. She'd never ever seen Will look this agitated or unsure of himself.

'I'm sorry about the other day, Mayu. I think you gave me as much of a shock as I gave you when I saw you pass out like that. I couldn't believe how stupid I'd been. I'm going to change, I really am.'

Mayu gazed into the deep blue of his eyes. There was no doubt in her mind that he was telling her the truth. 'So it was just a joke? You did it without thinking?' she whispered.

'Yes. No. Sort of.'

Mayu stared at him. He made talking look as though it was painful.

'Maybe I did it to prove to myself once and for all that you didn't give a toss about me,' he said eventually. 'I should have asked you out at the bowling alley. I was up for it, but when it came to the crunch I blew it. My mates were wetting themselves behind me, and you and your mate were looking at me as if I had some kind of contagious disease . . .' He gave a deep sigh and shrugged his shoulders.

'I'm sorry.' Mayu felt awful. She just hadn't thought what it must be like for him. 'I thought maybe your mates were daring you to come over for a laugh,' she murmured.

Will shook his head. 'I had to bribe them to go there that night, but as I was walking over to you I was thinking: What are you doing this for? You're mad. She's made it plain from the start that she can't stand you and you get on her nerves. And I bottled out.'

'I'm sorry,' said Mayu. 'If only you'd said something sooner.'

'I didn't know sooner, did I? Being the idiot I am I thought it was funny to play jokes on you. All the other waitresses know what I'm like and they don't react any more. You were different.'

'Stupid,' said Mayu.

'No. I'm the one that's stupid. I should have realised earlier what you meant to me, how I was racing into work to be near you, and how seeing you laugh brightened my whole day.'

'Oh.' Mayu's brain felt scrambled. This was all such a shock.

'But by then it was too late. I'd blown it. We seemed to be getting on OK, but I reckoned you'd just decided to humour me. You never let me get too close. Your mates would come over and talk and ask me all sorts of things, but you just weren't interested.'

'I was. I am.' Mayu looked up at him in confusion. 'I just can't be like them. It takes me longer to get to know somebody, but that doesn't mean I don't care.'

A slow smile formed on Will's face and Mayu felt a strange stirring in her stomach. She realised it was happiness.

'What would have happened if I'd asked you out?'

Mayu's heart juddered against her ribcage. 'Why don't you find out?' she whispered.

'God, girl, you don't make it easy, do you?' he said, but he was still smiling. 'So will you . . .?'

'Will I what?'

'You know . . . will you go out with me . . .?'

'OK.' She smiled back at him.

'OK?' He came over, cupped both his hands around her chin and stared deep into her eyes. It was the most romantic thing anyone had ever done. 'You're not joking?' he asked softly.

'No. Are you?'

'No. And I *am* going to change, Mayu. I'm going to stop messing around so much.'

'I don't want you to change, Will. Just give me a bit of notice next time you're thinking of stabbing yourself, OK?'

'I'm sorry, Mayu. I'll never hurt you like that again.'

'You'd better not.' Happiness was making her giddy. She held on to the front of his uniform while the rest of the storeroom spun away and went out of focus. Only Will was solid and real. His face came closer and closer to hers, blotting out everything else.

'I've wanted to do this for a long time,' he murmured, as his lips hovered over hers.

Mayu looked into his eyes. They were the colour of a summer sky as they sparkled down at her. Nothing could be as special as this moment. She would remember it for ever.

'What's going on? Why can't I open this door? Is Mayu there?' The hammering on the storeroom door, Mrs Emmanuel's yelling, and Will's deep groan gradually penetrated Mayu's consciousness.

'I've kidnapped her,' he shouted, and Mayu's eyes opened wide.

'What?' screeched Mrs Emmanuel.

'I said the door seems to have jammed, Mrs E.'

'What's she doing in there? There's a restaurant full of customers outside.'

♥ 151 ♥

Mayu heard Mrs Emmanuel's voice, but somehow the importance of what she was saying didn't seem to register. She began to wonder if she was dreaming, and she held on more tightly to Will. He smiled down at her and she felt the resonant thud of his heart under her hand. This was no dream.

'She was helping me to find a packet of chicken lips in the freezer,' said Will.

Mayu buried her face in his chest in case she giggled. His uniform smelt of herbs and spices and a faint trace of deodorant. It was a unique smell. Exactly like Will.

'A packet of what?'

'You know. That new ingredient we're trying out for the kids' menu.'

'If this is one of your jokes, Will . . .'

'You're getting me mixed up with somebody else, Mrs E. Now if you don't mind, it's been nice talking to you, but I need all my concentration for getting this lock open.'

He turned back to her with a grin. 'I think we've been rumbled,' he said. 'I don't think we've got much time.' And then his arms folded around her, he drew her close, and they both discovered just how special a kiss could be. As his lips pressed firmly against hers, Mayu realised how much she'd misunderstood him. But there was no mistaking his message now. She was the one he wanted, he cared about her, and he made her feel so good.

With her own kiss she tried to show him how she felt, and she thought she succeeded. Afterwards he gave a great sigh of contentment and snuggled into her neck, sending shivers of pleasure running all the way down to her toes.

Mayu felt she was going to burst with happiness. The shelf of pickles was digging into her back and would probably leave a permanent ridge there. She didn't care.

Mrs Emmanuel was going ballistic outside, and they'd both probably lose their jobs. She didn't care.

It was a great summer.

J·17
Subscribe now!

Get your fave mag delivered to your door every blimmin' month for a year and never miss a copy! How? Simply complete your details and return this coupon with your payment to *J17* Subscriptions Department, Tower House, Sovereign Park, Market Harborough, Leicestershire LE16 9EF.

☐ I enclose a cheque/postal order made payable to *J17* magazine for £19.20 (UK rate)

Please debit my Access/Visa/Amex/Diners

☐☐☐☐☐☐☐☐☐☐☐☐☐☐☐☐☐☐

Expiry date_____ Signature _____

Date_____

Name _____

Address _____

_____ Postcode _____

Or phone the Subscriptions Orders Hotline
01858 435339
Between 9.30am and 5.30pm Monday to Friday

Source code WA 1A
Offer code A12